Encounter

By

Alana Lorens

Suspense Thriller

Published by
Dragonfly Publishing, Inc.

ENCOUNTER

Suspense Thriller

Paperback Edition
EAN 978-1-941278-96-3
ISBN 1-941278-96-5

Hardback Edition
EAN 978-1-941278-97-0
ISBN 1-941278-97-3

eBook Edition
EAN 978-1-941278-98-7
ISBN 1-941278-98-1

Published in the United States of America by
Dragonfly Publishing, Inc.
Website: www.dragonflypubs.com

* * * * *

Acknowledgements

A ton of thanks to editor Terri Branson who bailed me out of my own mess. With hopes of a continuing partnership in our golden years.

* * * * *

Quote

"Any coward can be a peacekeeper! In fact, that comes to one naturally. But they are blessed, the peacemakers...and all those who know the difference." — Criss Jami, Healology

* * * * *

CHAPTER 1

Inez Suela huddled in the small box truck, in the corner nearest the door, stealing every breath of fresh air she could before the driver closed them in. Too many of them in here, too many. Once the door closed, she didn't know how she'd breathe.

Thirty-nine Mexicans had paid the driver, the *coyote*, thousands of pesos to transport them across the border to New Mexico. She had starved herself and dressed in rags to save through three lean years of meager wages. But she'd had enough to take a chance, to 'roll the dice', as they said in the American Las Vegas. Tonight was the night.

Even the money guaranteed nothing.

Others, who'd tried to make it and failed, said perfect timing might avoid being caught or turned back. Many had lost friends or relatives who'd attempted to cross the Arizona desert border on foot. The summer heat reached to 120 degrees, and you could die from lack of water and heat exhaustion. The winters weren't much better, as harsh weather in the mountains stole lives away.

March, though. March seemed a time with the best chance of success. Or so Uncle Ramon had promised. He'd sent several brothers north over the years, and the money those *norteños* returned to their families was three times what they'd earn if they had worked at home.

Most of those who chanced the border were men. It was hard, and they had responsibilities. But more and more women tried, sometimes with their children. Several of Inez's friends had been caught and deported, returning with their dreams deflated.

Some made it.

In big cities with large immigrant communities, one more Mexican was hard to track. It could be done.

Inez was single, and strong, and very determined. She believed.

She just had to not think about it too hard, leaving behind everything she knew. Including the man she could never have.

The trip would be a day or more, due to the roundabout route off the main roads, avoiding the main roads and the Border Patrol. This coyote had a reputation, though, one that said he placed his people. She trusted him—as much as she trusted anybody.

The coyote said a man named Davi Pilar would be waiting at the halfway mark to take them to St. Louis. She knew him, Davi.

He had wanted to marry her once. She'd denied him because he never bathed and he smelled of nasty unfiltered cigarettes. He'd left town, become a *norteño*, too. What would he say when he saw her?

Inez's aunt and a cousin had lived in the northern end of St. Louis more than five years. They sent money home for the rest of her aunt's children. Her cousin Juan drove a two-year old pickup truck with a new stereo deck. Perhaps she, too, could find a good life.

She didn't know the other travelers, save one. Rafael Diego sat across from her, hunched against the wall. He was a big man, not fat, with thick black hair and an easy smile that had faded in recent weeks. He'd left his wife and five children back in their village south of Juarez. Rafael could no longer find work at the *maquiladoras,* the factories that had come from the American side, using cheap Mexican labor to supply American profits. Not knowing what else to do to feed his family, he'd opted for the gamble as well.

They'd traveled together to meet the truck after the Tuesday sunset. Once they'd paid over their money, they climbed into the dark, hearing voices of the others, catching a glimpse of them in the faint light from the front.

Her fingers combed through her shoulder-length hair, thin like Inez herself, an anxious habit since her childhood. But Rafael didn't look anxious. Rafael was a good man.

She knew him from the neighborhood, how he pitched in to help those in need or stood up for the rights of those oppressed. His wife was a lucky woman. Inez wished for such a man when she was ready for marriage. But now that she was twenty-three, past the age most young women in her town caught the eye of their future *marido*, she doubted she'd find someone like Rafael. *And the man she loved was already taken. She only had herself.*

When it seemed like no more could possibly fit in, the driver yanked a Padres baseball cap down low on his forehead. He barked orders to keep quiet. Then he slammed the back shut and they rumbled up the road.

They were on their way to America.

* * * * *

CHAPTER 2

Escaping the catty women in the bar, Teo Haroun stepped into the small airport terminal at Santa Fe. His attention caught in the web of art stretching along the walls in shades of terra cotta, gold and turquoise. The tints matched the hues of the land outside the wide windows, a brilliant blue sky, red-brown desert sands and the grayed purple of mountains in the distance. It was an alien and mysterious landscape, open and drenched in color.

A far cry indeed from the gray and windy scene left behind at Chicago Midway, a bleak repetition of the days through the current winter. Teo drew warmth into his aching bones. As he approached forty-three, his tall, toned frame suffered unwelcome aches and creaks, though his café-au-lait skin was smooth. On a good day, he could pass for a man in his early thirties. But there were fewer and fewer good days.

High-pitched laughter from the bar drove him closer to the window. He worked with these people, competent lawyers in his firm, specializing in patent and computer law. But he would call none of them his friend.

Teo spied senior partner Mitchell Kadeen coming from the gate, cashmere coat draped carelessly over one arm as he walked with a long stride born of fifty-plus winters on the ski slopes of the world. Mitch stopped to lecture some unfortunate on the other end of his cell phone conversation, referring to documents in his Italian calfskin briefcase. Sharp parting words preceded his shoving the phone into his pocket.

Teo admired him, and he wasn't alone. Women often turned to look as Mitch walked by, hair leaning to more salt than pepper, handsome enough to play a soap opera tycoon. He stood tall, deeply blue eyes crinkled at the corners as he grinned, waving a locker key.

"I know, I know. I said no phones for the retreat. I'm leaving it here."

"And your files?" Teo's large dark eyes, a genetic gift from his Egyptian mother, studied the thick briefcase. His tone teased, soft silk compared to the edgy attacks of the women waiting inside, armed with their Cosmopolitans and white wine.

"Locked away before we leave the building. I swear. Sasha will just have to hold the fort on this one for a week." Mitch's smile faded, rueful.

"I know I've been a tyrant about this. But Judy insists if the six of us are to make the retreat work, we need to give it our full attention."

"Oh, I agree. Actually I've been looking forward." Teo nodded his head in the direction of the bar. "She's still trying to sell the experience to the others. They aren't as...shall we say, adventurous?"

Mitch sighed. "I can guess the ringleader."

Teo just smirked, returned his gaze to the view outside.

The idea of the retreat intrigued Teo from the beginning. Because of the disparate nature of the firm, two partners each in Arlington, Denver and Chicago, tradition dictated a group meeting at least once a year. This year, one of the Denver partners had suggested something other than their usual lush digs at a luxury hotel in a major city.

She'd come across the Sherman Ranch, five hundred acres of wilderness and a few communal style buildings west of Taos. The "in" thing for corporate groups, she'd suggested, was a professional course in team-building, to help the group learn about and come to depend on each other and their shared goals. She had rented the ranch for a week and hired Harmonics Inc. to lead them. Two hours from now, the 'adventure' would begin.

Laughter came from the bar again, and Mitch's shoulders squared up. "Cattrin here yet?"

"In there." That was one of the reasons Teo'd left, holding no love for Mitch's Arlington office mate.

Mitch grumbled. "She texted me she spent last evening art-shopping Canyon Road." He checked his phone, then glanced outside where the dark blue van awaited. "She'd better have shipped whatever she got back to Tyson's Corners. There's no room on the van for any fluffery."

Teo mulled several responses. "You're the boss."

"It's good to be the king. Isn't that what they say?" The twinkle in Mitch's eye belied the tightening of his jaw. He glanced at the doorway to the bar. "*She* in there?"

"Annie?" Teo replied, with a slow nod.

A deep breath signaled Mitch's reluctance for this particular face-to-face. "It should be a rule: Never stay in business with your ex-wife."

Teo let irony sink into his tone. "Not likely."

He had a solid work history, he was a rainmaker, and he was very circumspect, but after he'd been outted several years before—by one of the aforementioned catty females—it had become clear there would never be a wife. Or perhaps even companions.

Not anymore.

Mitch, on the other hand, was always seen with attractive young women, or so the society columns said. His latest office protégé was a constant topic of fractious bitchiness in the Chicago office Teo shared with the ex-wife in question.

As if summoned by his thoughts, Annike Lorant appeared in the wide doorway to the bar, her cool Scandinavian gaze hunting a target. Zeroing in on Mitch, she crossed her arms. "You finally made it."

"Annie. It's good to see you." Mitch moved close, pecked his former wife's cheek politely.

"Of course it is." Annike smiled more warmly than Teo expected as she squeezed Mitch's free hand. She winked at Teo over Mitch's shoulder, then drew Mitch inside the room of sparkling glasses and polished wood. "Come on. The others are waiting."

Teo counted his lucky stars that he didn't have to follow them, not just yet. *Much more peaceful out here. And less treacherous.*

Mitch and Annike had formed Artotech in the mid-1980s with several law school friends. Twenty years together had slowly choked the life from their jet-set marriage, but they still shared the firm. Annike was a great lawyer, her courtroom presence astounding. From the moment she started to speak, she cradled the judge in the palm of her hand.

Her flamboyance, however, carried over into her personal life. The break-up of the marriage played out like a Shakespearean tragedy on the firm's stage. Annike fled Arlington for Chicago, where she sulked like an injured dog for several months before she found her way again.

Teo was sympathetic, knowing both strong personalities, approving of her instinct to separate physically as well as legally. They were adults, for heaven's sake, entitled to their drama, since they surely worked too many hours to stock up on Jerry Springer and *Grey's Anatomy.*

But he'd since noted petty little machinations, conspiracies between Annie and Cattrin to keep her informed of Mitch's every movement, who he dated, who he hired. That, Teo hated. As far as he was concerned, personal lives should be private.

Teo took his carry-on bag to the sleek dark blue extended-bed van that waited, front and rear air conditioning pumping full blast. Polka-beat Mexican music issued from the CD deck.

A wiry man with Spanish features stacked pieces of luggage behind the rear seat, delivering a quiet monologue punctuated with obscenities. Teo didn't understand much of what he was saying, but between the bad words and the tone, he got the basic gist. *Greedy Americans.* True, the large pile of suitcases seemed like a grandiose amount of "stuff" for a week, even for six of them.

"Hello," Teo said. "Are we going to manage all this?" He set his bag on the front seat, marking his territory.

"It's impossible," the driver groused as he capitulated to the inevitable and radioed for a car top luggage carrier. Teo grinned and the man relaxed, reflected the smile. "What can you do, eh?"

"Go with the flow, my friend." Teo walked behind the van into the street, feeling the sun on his face. So long since it had been warm in Chicago. Here, March was nearly sixty degrees. After four months of bitter winter, it felt glorious. He took a deep breath, closed his eyes.

Moments later, tires squealed. A horn blared inches from Teo's thigh.

"Get out of the street!" an irritated male voice yelled. "Are you crazy?"

Teo jerked back to reality, found himself looking across the hood of a "Hello-Officer Red" Trans Am at a polo-shirted man with dark glasses and a jaunty black hat. "S-Sorry—"

"Sorry, my ass! Are you high? Get out of the fucking street!"

The Chicago partner squinted, studied the driver. "John?"

The driver swung out of the vehicle, lowered the shades a moment and looked at him. "Hey—Teo? Right? Oh hey, sorry, man. Damn glasses are really dark." The broad-shouldered man walked over, shoved a meaty hand in Teo's direction. "You okay?"

"Fine, fine." Teo shook his hand, released it when it was polite. He'd barely recognized the newest Denver partner, John Kirk Nicholas, responsible for most of the firm's West Coast clientele.

I hadn't realized he was such a jerk.

But Teo's friendly smile never wavered. He knew many men like John Kirk, confident of their own place in the world, cocky bastards who made sure they belonged to the "right" social groups and had the "right" opinions to get ahead, whether those opinions served the moral conscience or not. None of them was gay.

John Kirk turned to the van driver. "Hey, Pedro! Where can I park my rental?"

Teo stiffened as the driver gritted his teeth and pointed out the parking lot before turning back to his work.

The athletic Trans Am driver grinned at Teo and clapped him on the shoulder. "See you inside, pal." Climbing back into the car, he squealed his tires again and headed in the direction of the indicated lot.

In an attempt to offset John Kirk's bad impression on the driver, Teo helped Pedro unload the large suitcases and set them on the curb as a youngish man showed up with the requested car top carrier. "We're not all like that," Teo said apologetically.

The driver looked at him, cocked a brow. *"Gringos?"*

Surprised, Teo shook his head. "Lawyers."

"Ah." Pedro chuckled as he got back to work, and Teo retreated inside, feeling he'd been put in his place.

Interesting how we categorize and assign worth to ourselves by what we are, not who.

* * * * *

CHAPTER 3

Davi Pilar checked his box truck's oil, filled up with gas as he prepared for his upcoming run to New Mexico. This was the eleventh time he'd made the trip to bring his fellow countrymen to the land of milk and honey, and he got paid at least five thousand American dollars each time. Davi Pilar lived very well in his low-rent neighborhood. It was a good life.

Mocking himself, he snorted and wiped his hands on well-worn denim pants, then stooped down to measure the air in the tires of the truck he'd bought cheap at a used car auction. Once a Ryder truck, easily renowned as a successful trademark, then identified forever with death and destruction, thanks to that crazy gringo in Oklahoma City. Now it was a pretty white truck with a farm logo and the words "Two Brothers Trucking" painted on the rear door.

Too bad there's only one brother left.

Davi shoved aside the memory of his brother Tomàs, who hadn't made it when they'd crossed the border five years before. Some hotshot border vigilante had opened fire on the small group of men running across the desert. Tomàs had gone down hard. Davi, crouching behind a piñon, had called to him without response. It was clear his brother couldn't go on, whether he was dead or not, so Davi led the rest forward, leaving Tomàs there in the rusty sands. He'd heard later the body had been delivered to his mother. She hadn't forgiven him.

Davi picked at scabs on his thin, pock-marked face and waved to the local cop making his hourly cruise through the Citgo station parking lot. When the cop blew his horn, one of the girls inside came running with free coffee for the officer. The cop had no problem with him. The cop liked him. Of course the cop had no idea what Davi did for a living—he thought Davi hauled vegetables from the summer farms around the city.

Davi watched as the man took the coffee from the dark-haired girl. The cop's great big *comemierda* smile, his hand on her behind before she could walk away politely. Stupid Americans, they all thought Mexican girls were sluts. Head down in shame, the girl hurried back into the building.

As the cop drove by, he waved back and Davi forced a smile, though his insides twisted like a whirlpool. "You take care now!" he said in English hardly accented any more.

"Back at you, chief!" The black and white pulled out of the lot, radio buzzing.

Davi knew Estrella, the girl who worked inside. She was a good girl. Her parents had emigrated legally and owned this business as well as two others. They were legendary to their neighbors back in Zacatecas, where people spoke of them as if they ruled a minor empire.

He'd considered expressing his interest to her father. But he couldn't imagine that pretty Estrella's father would approve her marriage to a fifty-year-old man who might flash some cash, but had no obvious source of income.

And he would never ask her to her face. Not after what Inez Suela had done.

His first real love, he'd fallen hard for Inez when he'd worked at the hospital in Juarez as a janitor. The fresh-faced young nursing student was assigned to the second floor, and he made sure he cleaned during her shift so they could talk.

At first she'd been sweet. He'd brought her little presents and teased her. But when he began to get serious, she avoided him. He watched her every day, trying to gain her attention, but she'd act as if she didn't even see him. Worried he'd lose her, he followed her home one night. Breathless on the step, he asked her to marry him.

She answered, but it was all wrong. He admired her frank manner when she stood up to the doctors at the hospital, but when she turned it on him, it burned his ears like acid.

Her verbal assault flayed him into strips, laying out everything she hated about him and why she would never, never lie with him, even in his dreams. He saw pain in her eyes, but felt his own ten times worse. He crept away to drown his wounds with a bottle of smuggled whisky.

He whispered to the hospital interns that Inez had a sexual disease. No remorse chilled his heart as they taunted her, and one day she came no more to the hospital. While his pride was mollified, he still missed her wit, the strong face, her smile. Annoyed with himself, but more with her, he started making plans to go north.

Now, fueled by spite, he made the bimonthly run to bring more Mexicans to the States, a figurative flip of the finger to the Americans who rejected him, him and all his people. He was going to make a king of himself. They'd be sorry they weren't nicer to him. He'd show them.

Davi slammed the cap back on his gas tank, and climbed into the cab. He gunned the engine, and the truck rumbled out of the parking lot, headed for his small driveway. Two more days till he'd score again.

And just in time. The outstanding loan he'd taken from a pair of brothers came due the next week, with interest. They didn't care if he was white, black, Mexican, or Asian. They'd break his legs just the same.

* * * * *

CHAPTER 4

The ride was a rough one.

Inez found herself jostled and thrown into her neighbors often, but a soft apology was always met with understanding. Already achingly lonely, she tried to put the passing miles and the family she was leaving out of her mind. Her aging parents; she had tried to provide for them as she could. She'd even studied nursing at Juarez General Hospital with a grant from the *Fundación Mascareñas*, but when she wasn't working, she had nothing to share with her parents. She quit before she finished the program, partly because of the money. Partly because of Davi Pilar.

Her parents chastised her. They protested they were happy in their poverty.

"All we need is each other," her mother insisted.

Other family members had gone ahead to the *Estados Unidos*, or *El Norte*, as others said it. Besides her family in St. Louis, Inez had an aunt in Indiana, an uncle in Colorado, who had sent some letters over the years. Maybe she'd find them, if things didn't work out in St. Louis. Anything but going back.

She clung to her goal, the same as the others in this crowded truck—getting somewhere they could earn enough money for themselves, and perhaps their families, to survive, to have a life worth living, away from the grasp of dust and killing poverty.

The women too, had another incentive: freedom.

In America, women were not second-class citizens, restricted pieces of property. In America, a Mexican woman could drive a car, even in the small towns. She could have a husband who believed she was equal, who would share the household chores and the raising of the children. She could do what she wanted without the old *brujas* of the village giving her those looks.

If a woman was pretty enough, or talented enough, she could be famous, like Selena or Shakira or Jennifer Lopez, who Inez watched faithfully in the motion pictures. America had many opportunities.

But Inez held no illusions she would ever be like those women. She would still have to work, and work hard, the rest of her life.

As the truck trundled north, the smell of the nervous, close-packed bodies got stronger. Her back on the metal side of the truck was chilled. It was getting colder. Perhaps it would snow. That would be a treat—in Juarez it didn't snow often. She remembered as a child seeing the small white flakes falling from the sky, such a special occasion.

Her freedom and snow... forever linked in her mind.

She shoved the small cloth bag she carried behind her, blocking the worst of the cold. It wouldn't be long now.

The others hummed, whispered, snored as the miles passed. Sleep would make the time go more quickly. She maneuvered herself to a slightly warmer position, crossed her forearms across her bent knees, and laid her cheek on her arm, willing herself to the escape of slumber.

* * * * *

CHAPTER 5

When the group gathered on the curb next to the van, Teo was glad he'd staked out that seat in the front.

Round trip service to the ranch left them without a vehicle. Mitch insisted people leave their cell phones and laptops behind as well. *I want one hundred percent focus on our teamwork*, he'd said.

People weren't happy.

Judy Norell, the head attorney in Denver, directed people in her usual efficient way. Where a woman more vain would have opted for contacts, Judy chose tortoise-shell framed glasses that hid her bright brown eyes. The brunette had interesting features, but no one would have called her pretty. The mother of two teenaged boys, she dressed comfortably in a yellow *Explore New Mexico* sweatshirt and jeans. After cancer had killed her husband six months earlier, she'd volunteered for more and more partnership duties to fill her hours, including organizing this venture, but it hadn't changed her down-to-earth nature.

Judy leaned close to Mitch. "So how does it feel to be revolutionary?" she asked in a low-pitched but pleasant alto. "The loss of the ladies' perks. No facials and massages this year. It's making then a little...restless."

Mitch frowned. "Maybe it wasn't such a good idea."

She reached out to touch Mitch's arm in reassurance. "No, the level of sniping since we've arrived shows I was right. They're worse than my two kids. We see ourselves as individuals, not as a team. In the new century, we've got to compete with other firms, not with each other."

"Exactly." Mitch smiled tightly, pointedly avoiding Annike's gaze.

Teo cleared his throat over the awkward moment, peering inside the van. It seated twelve. *Six attorneys, plus the driver waiting to climb in.* "At least there's plenty of space."

Judy peered inside, doubt creeping into her voice. "Not really. Adding the trainers and their equipment, it'll be a tight over-friendly squeeze. By the way, Mitch, they called and said they'd be here by eleven. They're piggybacking in from a gig in Dallas."

"They're not here by eleven-O-one, they'll be making their own way out to the Ranch," Mitch warned. Coiled tight, he walked over to John

Kirk and jumped into a discussion of the vagaries of March Madness.

"They'll be here," Judy said to no one in particular, then pulled out her cell and dialed, walking away into the shade of the terminal entryway.

* * *

The Harmonics trainers arrived with three minutes to spare and four large suitcases, most of which contained their equipment. Teo thought the van driver was going to have a coronary.

"Here, I'll help with that, man," said the athletic young male half of the pair, who introduced himself as Will Starlin. He climbed onto the top of the van and tied the suitcases down as aerodynamically as possible. Muscles rippled under his Tony Hawk T-shirt, and his dark brown hair was spiked like that of a street punk.

"Last trip we had to fit all this in a Geo. Unreal!"

"Yeah. I think Will was driving with his knee." Zanna Michaels giggled as she helped hand the bags up. She was pigtailed, blonde and looked like a member of the U.S. gymnastic team. Several of the men couldn't take their eyes off her skin-tight jeans.

Judy took charge of the twenty-something pair, answering their questions on the run as Mitch barely suffered an introduction before he barked orders to load into the van.

"Come on, folks, we'll be out there a week. Lots of time for chit-chat then. Saddle up!"

Teo slipped into the seat he'd appropriated earlier, catching glares from partners forced to sit shoulder-to shoulder in the back.

The group split along gender lines, just like an elementary school playground. Annike slipped into the rear-most seat with Cattrin Odeon, who was built as compact as a wren, with the same birdlike mannerisms. Of Filipino descent, Cattrin's new affectation was Europeanizing people's names to sound cultured. There was "Giuditta" and "Mitchello" and "Teodoro" just to start.

Judy joined the trainers in the next seat forward, taking the seat closest to the door. They carried on conversation, hardly missing a beat, already planning strategy for the weekend.

Mitch, looking uncomfortable but not entirely unhappy, slid in behind Teo, face flushed like he'd forgotten to take his blood pressure medicine. Directly behind the driver was Mr. Trans Am, who took every opportunity to steal a look at the rear end of the blonde cheerleader when she got excited and scooted up—which she did a lot. His attention didn't go unnoticed; his efforts to flirt doubled. Teo smirked and turned his interest to the front.

The driver didn't wait for direction to leave, clearly feeling the pressure-cooker nature of the trip. As he took a left onto the Veterans Memorial Highway, he smiled at Teo, revealing very white but broken teeth

"Have you been to New Mexico before, *señor*?"

Teo took a last glance in the sun visor mirror at those in the back, and snapped it closed. "I've passed through a few times. I grew up in California—San Diego," he added. He studied the driver's rough face. "Are you a native?"

The middle-aged man grinned. "No. I'm an alien."

"Not from Roswell, then?" Teo nodded with a self-mocking smile, feeling the need to make himself seem less a...*gringo*.

The driver laughed. "No, no. I am first from Mexico. Came here ten years ago with my wife."

"Did you—" Teo tried to think of a diplomatic way to ask. "Come...um...."

"Cross over?" The man chuckled and nodded. "It is the way many begin here. We have established lives now, and green cards. But yes, we came across the back country."

America. The land of opportunity. Teo recalled similar stories about refugees who'd braved the waters of the Caribbean hoping to reach Miami's shores. Cubans were accepted for political asylum; simple economic oppression wasn't enough to extend the welcome mat for dark-skinned Haitians. So many were denied the dream, either dying in transit or being sent home by the U.S. government.

Yet that's why the Mexicans and Central Americans invaded the Southwest—job opportunities. And many of them stayed, too.

"Did you find it dangerous?" he asked over the buzz of conversation behind them. "We read a lot, but I suppose we can't understand what it's really like."

"It could have been. We didn't get caught." The man shrugged, watching the road signs pass. "*Estamos en las manos de Dios.*"

Teo looked at him curiously. "I'm sorry?"

He grinned. "God watched over us."

"I understand the immigration process is a real challenge. The government talks about amnesty, sometimes, when it's not ranting about building a wall. It would help, wouldn't it?"

Before the driver could answer, John Kirk leaned forward and interrupted. "Make all those fine people into taxpayers, wouldn't it?"

The driver's face clouded over. He shifted, then turned his full attention back to the road.

Teo shot John Kirk a look. "Not everyone is born to privilege and football scholarships," he said with a hint of tartness. "We could all stand to consider things from another point of view."

"And what have you done for the Great Unwashed of late, Mr. Graphic Arts specialist?" John Kirk scoffed.

Teo stopped short of a smirk. "Actually, last fall I worked with Windy City Habitat for Humanity to build a home on the west side. A single mother of five got her first house. It was pretty exciting."

Nonplussed, the Denver man's gaze fixed on Teo's manicured hands. "I-I had no idea."

"They have gloves, doll." He laughed softly. "I made a substantial financial donation from the office to cover Annike's share," he whispered.

Mitch chuckled as John Kirk retreated into his *New York Times*.

Teo glanced past the cheerleader's shoulder where Annike compared diamond jewelry with Cattrin in the back seat. He didn't begrudge their attachment to things. He loved things. He lived alone in a 15th floor apartment overlooking Lake Michigan, with a collection of Dialogica furniture from San Francisco. He loved the burgundy Lawrence sofa and the splash chairs in burnt orange. The interior was minimalist, each piece special, a splash of color against off white walls.

Several of his own paintings graced the walls, his favorite an acrylic on canvas of a pale green vase holding yellow lilies. The small balcony grew full of plants in the summer, a leafy profusion of greens and colorful blooms nearly concealing black rattan chairs and a tall glass-topped table. He cherished that space that protected and cushioned him from painful truths.

That was it. That was what counted. Each person worked hard to attain his best level of achievement and the rewards commensurate with that. Some people wanted diamonds or a Trans Am. Others just wanted a living wage and a little bit of comfort.

"So do we get any free time?" Will asked. "There's a radical bike trail that winds for miles along the Rio Grande Gorge—totally awesome!"

"Tell her about the Earthships," his perky companion blurted on his heels.

Teo paused to listen in, loosening his seatbelt and warily negotiating the few free inches of footspace in the front to shift around. His foot still tapping to the beat, the driver turned down the polka music slightly.

Starlin was fired up. "Oh, man, yeah! There's a whole subdivision, it's like half underground. All you see is the sun and sky reflecting off the glass windows, like skylights? The walls are made of car tires filled with dirt, sealed up. That gives you thermal mass. It's perfectly suited for the desert, like old adobe brick. But it's even better, because it uses recycled materials. The southern faces of the houses are still open, so people can get in. It's all passive solar heating and light. Really environmentally sound."

"Do they give tours?" Teo asked.

Will's hazel eyes were warm with enthusiasm. "The main center's in Taos, so there's a showroom or something. But the houses are owned by private people."

"Probably not a lot of use for solar heating units in Chicago," Judy teased.

"Probably not." Teo smiled with near-perfect teeth at the two young people, thinking they were bright and vivacious and full of color. He'd been that way once, hadn't he? Before the world had caught up with him.

When Will and Zanna flitted to a new topic, Teo moved his attention to the spectacular view ahead. The bright colors and terra cotta of Santa Fe faded to red-tinged desert rocks against the purple haze of the Sangre de Cristo mountains on the east, and the San Luis hills on the north, toward Colorado.

The conversation blurred into murmurs. The small towns they passed had Spanish names like Espanola and Ojo Caliente, where the old mineral springs signs still welcomed visitors. The skies north began to stack up with gray-lined clouds, leaving the azure heavens behind. "Is that rain coming in?" he asked the driver.

"Snow, they said. A lot by the end of the week. Strange, but not unheard of this time of year. It happens like that sometimes, blows in all at once. But you'll be nice and warm, not to worry."

Teo nodded, his thoughts returning to the retreat. Judy had promised outdoor activities, challenging the partners, a sedentary group working mostly ten-hour days. The scheduled activities would be revealed on site. Though she wasn't a malicious person, Judy seemed to derive some pleasure from the rumblings in the back seat.

You'd hate for any of them to break a nail.

All the same, he was proud of his work in the community, something more than just what served his own professional ambition. As the van pulled under the rough wooden arch that marked the entrance to the ranch, Teo smiled. *Saving the world isn't such a bad objective after all.*

* * * * *

CHAPTER 6

The crunch of the van's tires on the gravel as it rounded the final turn to the ranch's main building made Jake Patrin check his watch.

Ten minutes early. Damn it.

He'd wanted to be out front to greet them, but he was still in the back staff quarters sealing a window frame before the blizzard came in. He muttered and set the caulking gun aside to go orient the newcomers.

He stripped off his dirty red plaid flannel shirt as he went through the north kitchen, tossing it in a closet after wiping what he could of the thick white paste from his hands. He dragged a black comb through what was left of his hair, then tucked it back in his jeans pocket as he grabbed a new flannel and moved on to the lobby. The polished wood floors and minimally-furnished rooms echoed his cowboy-booted footsteps.

He hurried, but he didn't run. "Built for comfort, not for speed," he muttered.

Story of my life these days.

The age of thirty-five had impacted Jake like no other in his life. His wife had divorced him and he'd lost a good job in King City. Worse, a collision with a Mack truck late one night when he'd been driving too long had stuck him in the hospital for three months, left him in constant pain controlled by serious doses of Oxycontin and other medications. But the drug had become his master, had taken over for a while. Almost a year later, he'd kicked the narcotic, but he still struggled to leave behind the addiction.

That's why he was here, living in the middle of nowhere. Here he could stay clean and sober. Weekly trips to Santa Fe (or more often, if he needed) hooked him up with a middle-aged male Alcoholics Anonymous group that helped keep him sane. His sponsor was an old Indian, John White Horse, who'd fought his own good fight for nigh on forty years. John took no bullshit. He was a good friend and good support.

Jake opened the turquoise-painted front door to the 6000-square-foot main house and stepped outside. People crawled from the blue extended van like cockroaches, quickly scattering, stretching, rebuilding their personal space. *Dressed better than roaches, though,* Jake noted with a hint of irony.

"Welcome to the Sherman Ranch!" he called out. They glanced at him, took in his drab appearance. Most dismissed him. It didn't hurt; he was used to it. He was no big-city doorman with a heavy wool coat and a fancy top hat, that was for sure. A couple of the women, what he'd call *High maintenance types*, eyed the sandy exterior of the building and the lack of yard with horror.

Jake knew better. That carefully-cultivated rustic appearance was skin-deep. The ranch might be rural but it was quite modern. Solar panels provided the majority of the power that kept the place warm and heated the water, though there was gas to back it up. The facility's eight bathrooms all had radiant heat, and they enjoyed satellite TV and high-speed computer access in the main lounge. The hot tub ran just fine, and with ten separate sleeping areas, guests had plenty of privacy.

Pete, the driver, gave him a short nod and went straight for the back of the van. *That was a bad sign.* The driver got a lot of the gigs hauling folk out to the ranch. If he wanted this batch out of his vehicle that fast, there was a good reason. If it was really bad, he wouldn't stick around for coffee once the tourists were unloaded. *We'll wait for the update.*

A comfortable-looking brunette with glasses slid out of the back seat and walked over to him with a smile. "Hi, I'm Judy Norell. We spoke on the phone."

His personal radar pinging off Pete's, he remained cautious as he shook her outstretched hand. "Jake Patrin. I'll be your...host, I guess, while you're here for the week. Your food and other supplies arrived on Tuesday, got it all stashed in the main kitchen. Bedrooms are made up like we discussed, linens out." He warmed as she smiled with satisfaction.

"Wonderful. We appreciate the accommodations you've made, Mr. Patrin." She looked along the terra cotta front to the building with interest. "I can't wait to explore the place. Your website had great photos." She leaned a little closer. "I haven't really told the rest of them much about it. It will be part of the adventure."

The amusement in her eyes as she glanced back at the fancy ladies won Jake over. She seemed like good, plain people. "Looks like the weather will hold on a couple of days. If you've got outdoor plans, best handle them before Wednesday. Forecast for the weekend's unstable, but it looks like a winter snow dump."

"We'll do that."

Jake looked over the others, picking out the two kids from the task-setting company. "I got your schedule. You need room assignments?"

"I have that handled." Judy pulled out a paper and turned to the others.

"Mr. Patrin has promised me the rooms are already." She tore off little tickets from the paper and handed them out while Pete finished taking down the last suitcases, with the help of the hippie-looking kid.

"Three men, three women," Judy said, moving into the crowd. "Two rooms."

"We have to *share* a room?"

The aging blonde bombshell studied Judy a moment and turned her icy gaze on Jake. "Surely there's enough space that the senior partners can at least have their own rooms."

Caught off guard, Jake shoved his hands in his worn pockets. Before he could open his mouth to speak, Judy rescued him.

"It's part of the exercise, Annie. We share rooms, mix up the offices. It'll be like camping." She smiled brightly as she handed out the rest of the paper slips. "You must have gone camping sometime in your misguided youth. Before you found Nordstrom."

As the blonde slowly un-bristled, Judy flicked her hands in the direction of the stack of bags the trainers had. "These two probably ought to be where they can organize all this stuff. Maybe down at the bunk room? You've got two rooms down there, don't you?"

A snicker came from the group of men stacking the luggage. Jake studied them a moment, overheard the big-muscled guy make a pointed whisper about sharing a room with the little blonde. The women ignored him, and Jake decided that might be the best policy.

The young couple seemed to accept their assignment with ready enthusiasm. Jake opted to take them in first, loading their multiple suitcases on a small cart for ease of transport. They crossed the lobby and the gray stone hallway, then turned left down a corridor that passed the rec room with its large screen television, shelf of cased DVDs and sparse bookshelf. A further left brought them out nearly to the front of the building again to adjoining rooms, each with two bunk beds and four small dressers. Navajo print blankets lay on the beds along with fluffy pillows. The trim around the windows and door was in dark wood, a contrast to the bleached white of the wall. The blankets were the one splash of color in the room; it was a place to sleep, nothing more.

"So. You two want—ah, one room or two?" Jake looked them over, tried to guess by the amount of familiarity between them. *Made a cute couple, they did.*

The little blonde giggled. "Oh, momma! We're not—I mean we just work together." She blushed. "Will, he's like my big brother."

The young man nodded. "Two rooms will be fine." He shifted the duffel bag he carried over his shoulder. It looked heavy.

"Right then. Miss, pick one. Son, you take the other," Jake said. He lifted the heavy cases off the cart and set them centrally located, letting them grab their own. He checked the schedule. "Judy says you're free till two p.m. Then you'll meet out in the ceremonial hut." He pointed out the window to a thatched roof pole structure. "Guess she'll take over from there."

"Thanks, man." The young kid with the spiky hair shook his hand warmly. "I'm Will, and this is Zanna."

Jake grinned. "You'll be pretty much able to keep to yourselves down here. My room's along the hall that way, along with the staff quarters." At their inquisitive look, he shook his head. "We don't have staff this session. Just me. I'm chief procurement officer, tour guide, handyman... you name it. Need anything, come see me."

"Yes, sir. Let's get the gear stowed, Zan. Then I want to go take a walk, check out that arroyo on the far side of the house." Will grinned. "The layout is awesome."

"Thanks. We like it," Jake said. "Let me head out and rescue some of the other folk. You kids get settled, okay?"

As they murmured assent and started organizing their things, he walked back to the lobby, pulling the luggage cart. The others had disappeared into the *casa;* he heard their voices echo down the west hall. Pete helped him load their suitcases onto the cart.

Jake grinned at the weary look on the driver's face. "Interesting group, eh, *amigo?*"

Pete snorted. "Not satisfied with anything. Big city *gringos.*"

"Hey, big city *gringos'* money keeps enchiladas on the table, right? You and me, pal, we work for a living." As he stacked the eleventh piece of luggage, he wondered exactly what these men and women thought they'd be doing for seven days that required all this. "How's Maria?"

"She's good, she's good." Pete smiled with his broken teeth. "Knitting for the grandbaby." He whipped out his wallet and shared pictures of a fat, dark-skinned infant. "Esteban Marrero-Nunez."

"Gonna be a ladykiller." Jake grinned and handed the pictures back with a hint of jealousy. His wife had left after twelve years, taken everything they owned, but they'd never had kids. He'd been on the road so often, it hadn't troubled him much. Except for times like this. He wished he had some pictures to flash around. *Something of himself to leave behind. Something to help strengthen his resolve during those moments when the cravings really tore at his gut.*

"Got time for coffee? Put a fresh pot on bit ago."

Pete looked at the van, his watch and then down the hall. "Better head back, my friend. *Bueno suerte.*" He shared a tired smile, then hurried out and hit the road.

That bad. Damn. It was gonna be a long week. Jake rubbed his forehead and went for a cup of that coffee all alone.

* * * * *

CHAPTER 7

Inez woke when an argument broke out in the front end of the box. Two young men fought over space. At least that's what they were shouting about. Inez suspected that wasn't what the fight really meant. They'd been driving for a long time, it was hard to tell in the dark how long, it was cold and close, and tempers were flaring.

A small flashlight went on across from her, and she looked into the face of Rafael Diego. He smiled. "*Que tal?*"

As if it wasn't obvious... She smiled at his irony. "*Nada interesante.*"

He laughed. "*Para mi tampoco.*" He winked and shined the light at the troublemakers as the coyote banged on the front of the box, yelling at everyone to shut up. Inez caught the hot dark glare of a young *cholo*, barely a man. Angry at first, he saw her look and did an about-face, made kissy-lips in her direction. He smiled, clearly flirting with her. She thought about it for a moment—but only a moment.

I could be his sister, his older, wiser sister. Still smiling at his coy antics, she stiffly settled back into her former position, cramped from the crush of the others. The older man to her right complained about the cold; his woman shushed him and gave him some food from a small bag.

The whiff of spiced meat made Inez's stomach rumble. She dug in her pockets for some crackers she'd stashed there. She hadn't brought much in the way of food, not for the day's ride they'd been promised. Others had obsessed over their supplies earlier, the old mamas seemingly ready to feed a whole family for Sunday dinner.

Inez was used to dealing with a lot less. Even when she'd had a good job by her neighborhood's standards, she'd carefully saved half of what she earned for her mother each week. The older woman scolded her for being thin, but never refused the donation.

This move would save them both, Inez was sure of it. Her mother's neighbor had agreed to watch out for her, promised Inez that she would want for nothing. Inez's mother had cried, embraced her daughter and given her a gold cross that had belonged to her grandmother. "*El dios le bendice, mi hija. Venido véame pronto.*"

Inez doubted she would return home any time soon. With a sigh, she stretched what limbs she could and leaned back. If there was a light for her at the end of the tunnel, it was that perhaps she would be able to send for her mother someday, and care for her once again, in a manner that her mother deserved after raising three children on next to nothing.

Soon she'd be in the *Estados Unidos*...hopefully for good.

* * * * *

CHAPTER 8

Teo made it to their multi-bunked room first, but when John Kirk arrived, he spread his possessions across the largest share of the room. More interested in exploring the new venue than getting territorial, Teo tucked his most private items safely inside a sock and left the room.

The view out every window mesmerized him. The stark expanse of sand and scrub was a complete about-face from the damp mistiness of San Francisco, the tall skyscrapers of Michigan Avenue, the tropical lushness of Miami. The way the horizons faded into smoke, the ashy, dry emptiness, felt like a quickly-dissipating dream.

He continued to the long, wide lounge. A large, professionally-braided rag rug centered the large room with tones of turquoise, gold and burnt orange. Wooden Adirondack-style chairs covered with overstuffed cushions in red and gold were placed as if waiting for intimate conversation. A fire roared in the brick fireplace on the south wall, its mantle and frame covered in tile that echoed the colors of the rug.

The kitchen adjoined the lounge, connected by a wide door frame with no door and a six-foot pass-through, where a basket of bottled water had been set on its beige Formica counter. He peeked into the small pantry, finding it well-stocked. Certainly no one would starve during the upcoming week.

Voices followed him into the lounge, Judy's distinctive alto and the young woman from the Harmonics team.

"So who was the guy with the shades? He's hot. It's a small group, right? So we'll all get to know each other better." The girl grinned, caught a glimpse of herself in the wide mirror over the fireplace and adjusted her pigtails.

Judy laughed. "Guy with the shades? Didn't everyone have glasses?" She took a bottle of water off the counter.

"You know. The *one*. Sitting behind the driver."

"Ohh. John Kirk Nicholas. He's a partner in my office."

Teo raised an eyebrow. *And probably old enough to be your father.*

"A partner. Oooo." Zanna's smile never faded. "So. Lawyers. That is so cool. I mean, you must have had to go to school, like, forever to be that."

Judy caught Teo's eye and winked. "Well, maybe not forever."

Teo came in to join them. "When you're young, three years is a long time, Judy. Remember?"

Three years ago…a whole lifetime for me.

The other Harmonics kid came in. "Judy, how long until the opening ceremony?"

She checked her watch. "About forty-five minutes."

"Want to come out to the arroyo? I need to stretch my legs. We can brief you on our planned activities."

"Sure. I could use some fresh air. Teo, you want to come along?"

He considered it, but the thought of company right then didn't appeal to him. "No, thanks."

"See you soon." Judy took the youngsters in hand and crossed to the door at the far end of the room, then disappeared outside.

Teo continued to wander through the building, finding himself at a door opening onto a rough patio bounded by a four-foot adobe wall. A weathered wood picnic table staked out the far corner of the fifteen-foot square, a scrubby cactus in a terra cotta pot behind it. A red coffee can graced the table, half full of sand and burnt cigarette butts.

Still at first, a wild, pristine panorama, the view slowly came to life. A hawk flew overhead, dove into the sands. Other birds circled, landed. The breeze brushed the sparse green branches, sending them mildly rippling. He leaned his elbows on the wall, spotting Will, Zanna and Judy as they walked away from the main building, then disappeared from view in a scrub of piñon trees.

Letting the quiet flow into him, Teo accepted this moment for himself. He took a deep breath of the warm dry air, held its mysterious nature within, then released it with his tension and his negativity. He'd embraced meditative practice lately, creating brief, cleansing moments of serenity to give his body the encouragement it needed, in case the cosmos was up for the miracle Teo desired beyond all things.

Anything could happen.

It was his mantra. Repeating it, he found a tranquil mental state to relax until the gathering.

* * *

At the appointed hour, they filed out to the irregular hut, its weathered wood supports creaking as the wind brushed past, its thatched roof part of the natural landscape, too. Judy instructed them to form a circle, then she unwrapped a package on the table, setting aside the soft navy blue cloth.

"As part of the Western tradition, I thought we'd borrow an opening ceremony from native culture. We'll honor the Four Directions in the traditional way."

John Kirk Nicholas openly rolled his eyes, while the Harmonics team looked intrigued. Annike made some comment *sotto voce* to Cattrin. Teo's past was anchored in Christian ritual, not pagan, but he was open to new concepts—perhaps more than most of the teachings of his mother's church.

Judy lit the end of a bundle of sticks or dried grasses with a lighter. A bright braid of string hung down from the bundle, black, white, yellow and red. The embers were waved to brightness with a large white feather tipped in black. In a few minutes, the smoke from the burning leaves wafted around the closely-gathered group, its pungent smell vaguely reminiscent of marijuana. Mitch had been half-present while Judy spoke, but this perked up his attention and he raised an eyebrow. "Judy, what's—"

"Shhh. It's sage, Mitchell. Don't you remember the sixties?"

She walked the perimeter of the group, letting the smoke rise into the air, fanning the embers with the feather when they threatened to extinguish.

"Our thanks to the East, which brings the Fire each morning, to warm and sustain life."

Moving on, she stopped a quarter of the way around the circle. "Our thanks to the South, the home of the Earth, that which grounds us and feeds us."

Despite a pained look from Annike, she continued another quarter-round.

"Our thanks to the West, where lives the water which nurtures us and runs as blood through our veins." She waved smoke at those nearest her and continued on. "Our thanks to the North, home of the wind and air, bringing us the breath of life."

Back where she'd begun, she inhaled the scent of the sage and closed her eyes. "All we need, we have: fire, earth, water and air. May we use them wisely and generously for the greater good. Blessed be."

Life sounded so simple when reduced to those words, echoed readings from native peoples of a hundred years before. Just gratitude and appreciation for what you had been given, and the direction to protect and keep it. *Simple.*

Ceremony concluded, Judy invited them back inside for refreshments before they started their activities. Teo pondered the similitude of human experience. Whether caught in the modern world, buried in multi-tasking, fax, microwaves, cell phones and the constant demands of technology, or fighting to stay alive, hunting food and shelter in a time when a bite from a wild animal could kill...people were still people, with a basic need to be warm and safe.

Teo poured hot water over a green tea bag and watched Annike work the group. She moved like a panther, sleek and practiced, as though she always expected eyes on her. She paused just in the middle of the room, wearing skin-tight leggings and a slinky shirt in a pale teal that outlined her thin proportions and set off her Scandinavian features.

Mitch and John Kirk placated her need for attention, while Cattrin made small efforts to compete.

Better them than me. I keep her happy all year round. As for Cattrin, Teo only had one thought: *Little witch.*

The four took the most central chairs in the lounge. Judy spoke with the facility caretaker at the pass-through before she took a stool near the kitchen. John Kirk settled into his over-stuffed chair with a wink at Mitch. "Got to keep an eye on the boss man."

Mitch grinned back. "Better for me to keep an eye on you. Did you get that last set of drawings back to Premiere before you left?" His smile remained intact, but a trace of tension crossed his face as the inevitable business talk crept back in.

"Fed Exed them before three. They've been registered, sealed and recorded."

"Good. Very good."

Annike laughed in a low sultry tone, drawing everyone's eyes again. "Mitch, dear, as tightly as you're wrapped we should have brought a bag of charcoal along. You could stress them into diamonds to pay for the rental of this rustic little hovel."

Her tone was light, but her eyes held the same sharp tint as at the airport. She hadn't forgiven Mitch for everyone having to be here, or for anything else, probably, clinging to that grudge like a lifeline. *For how long?*

Judy tapped the counter lightly. "A bit of housekeeping?"

"Now we get to do housekeeping, too?" Annike's comment, delivered with lazy ennui.

Judy's smile lost none of its incandescence. "Not only are we following Harmonics' instruction for the exercises, we're also doing so by sharing quarters and being segregated from the world. We're miles from distractions, especially with all your electronics left behind."

She eyed them, steel firm behind the pleasant smile. "We haven't searched your bags, of course. We're counting on you as officers of the court."

At the mention of searching the bags, Teo stiffened. *Surely they wouldn't really do that. There had to be some privacy among adults.* He'd left his phone, his laptop and all his case data at home. Without them, he hoped to find a few moments of peace.

That wasn't what he had to hide.

"Work should be left behind, too." She assured them a phone existed on the premises. Artotech staff had the number, instructed to call only in case of extreme emergency.

""Breakfast and lunch will be on your own—wash up after yourselves. Mr. Patrin is here for the week, but it's clear in the contract he's not the maid, *or* your mother. We'll prepare dinner each night in groups. I'm passing around a sign-up sheet." She checked a list. "John and I will take tonight."

Mitch grinned from his fireside seat. "I got nachos and beer night covered."

A titter of laughter provoked Judy's smirk.

"Well, maybe the rest of you can be more creative. Here's a list of what's available to cook with. We've got beer, as Mitch said, but there's also an assortment of fine wines. We couldn't expect people to live in a completely primitive environment."

Judy waited until the babble over the papers settled down. "Now, I'd like to introduce the Harmonics team and let them take over."

She beckoned the two from their window seat. "Will Starlin has a degree in recreational therapy from Everest College in Portland, Oregon. He's a champion rock climber, and has been employed by Harmonics for three years. Zanna Michaels is new to Harmonics; she has her Bachelor's in physical education from Bowling Green State University in Ohio."

"She doesn't look like any gym teacher I ever had," John Kirk said, half under his breath. "Wonder if she teaches wrestling."

Teo frowned, hoping Mitch would point out the impropriety of the comment, but he only snickered, toying with a pencil and paper on the table, creating a to-do list in his slanted, stiff hand.

Judy cleared her throat, seeming determined to get through despite John Kirk's attitude. "They'll challenge us mentally and physically, beginning with exercises designed to reveal things about our team we might not know, even working beside them every day."

"What if we'd really rather not know everyone's deep, dark secrets?" Annike said.

"Are you afraid, Annie?" Mitch's voice was warmly amused. "Maybe they'll discover that crazy raccoon rocketing around in your head."

Annike gave her ex-husband a fake smile. "I'll bet they could learn a few shocking things about you, my love."

John Kirk led the chorus of catcalls. "Clipping, I'd say," he quipped. "Keep it up and you'll get a penalty."

Teo expected Will might be dismayed by the emotional temperature of the room, but seemed undaunted. *Good for him.*

Not all the law partners were pleasant people. John Kirk's behavior that morning, for example. Annike's temper tantrums were near-famous. Cattrin affected coming from money, but it was only a well-polished act. Around Annike and the other partners, she strived to be just as good, just as rich, just as blasé and unfeeling as any of them. *Like now.*

Will took a seat on a table and grinned at the group. "We've got several events planned, like Judy said. Mr. Patrin says they're expecting some snow by week's end. I'm sure it won't be much, not this time of year.

"We had a lot of options. Some traditional corporate challenges involve climbing across ravines, building human towers and all that. But based on the terrain here, we've decided to make the primary outdoor events geoteaming competitions." At a rumble of discontent, he waved a hand and looked at Judy. "I understand there's prizes."

"Anticipating objections, I used some of our budget to acquire gift certificates," Judy confirmed. "Spa weekends, golf outings, shopping sprees. But hopefully, some of you have enough pride to win just for bragging rights."

"Geoteaming is a competition like a treasure hunt," Will continued. "You'll be divided into teams, and assigned to find several caches hidden around the ranch."

Cattrin studied pearly white nails. "An Easter egg hunt. How professional."

"Actually, it's very techno-savvy," Zanna added. "The caches have varying points, so your individual score counts toward your team total. But there's a total team objective, too, so you have to work together for each goal. You'll have a GPS unit, two-way radios and aerial and topographical maps to help out."

"GPS? I have that in my car. I hardly need one here." Cattrin smiled at Will, somehow looking pixie-esque and coquettish. Was she flirting? Teo wondered. Or just trying to impress the other partners with her ability to patronize?

"Just like the one in your car." Will said. "This is a handheld version.

The addresses of the hidden boxes will be entered into your system, so you'll have to learn how to use it. We'll have a special session at seven a.m. tomorrow to show you.

"We'll have three geoteaming events. Zan and I will make sure the caches are in place, that you are trained to use the GPS, and then we'll be available to consult if necessary."

Sitting back with his tea, Teo thought it would be quite a challenge. *But if Will thought these partners would work together, he had a real surprise coming.*

"But tonight we have some easier exercises. Zanna?"

He turned to the blonde, who handed out 5x8 pads of paper and pens. "The first exercise is called Two Truths and a Lie. You write down three facts. Two should be true, and one a lie. Your friends will then guess which is which."

"Won't it be obvious?" Judy asked.

Zanna shrugged. "It's more fun if you dig deep for some outrageous things from your pasts, things they'd never believe you did. We've all done something pretty wild, right?"

Will turned a low-backed chair and straddled it. "I'll go first, so you can see how it's done." He grinned and thought a moment. "I was a linebacker on my high school football team. I have three sisters older than myself. My favorite food is green tea ice cream." He looked around expectantly. "So, which of those is a lie? Any takers?"

Teo smiled at Judy, who sat closest to him. "Well? He looks pretty athletic, huh?"

"Yeah. But he's more skateboard than scoreboard." She studied the young man curiously. "Green tea ice cream?"

"I had some once at a place in Pittsburgh, right down by where the three rivers meet," Teo said. "Absolutely the best. If he's had it, that's could well be true."

Little exchanges went on around the room, like their own. But what nagged at his mind was his own turn. *What could he offer that wouldn't reveal too much of the truth?*

"If you had sisters," Mitch called out, "they'd never let you wear your hair all spiky like that."

The others laughed with some sympathy.

"Do we get clues?" Cattrin asked.

"Nope. Cut and dried. Which is it? You can make a team guess if you want." He gestured at the group.

Judy finally volunteered a solution. "We'll vote. How many for the football star?" Teo raised his hand. "The sisters?" Mitch and John Kirk raised theirs, as did Judy. "The green tea ice cream?" The two other women weighed in on that one after a long moment during which Teo wondered if they would participate at all.

Tallying up, Judy smiled at Will. "Which is it?"

The young man grinned. "Well, I have four sisters, actually, but three are older. Green tea ice cream is the best Japanese dessert ever. But I've *never* played high school football." He pointed across at Teo. "Good call."

John Kirk leaned close to Annike. "Unfair. Teo's got an eye for the men."

Annike caught Teo's eye and shushed the Denver partner. Teo chewed the inside of his lip and doodled on his pad with his yellow pencil, letting the development of evolved geometric figures mend the insult in John Kirk's tone.

Judy smiled and sat on a rough-hewn end table. "Let's take five minutes to choose three things, then the dinner team should go first, give us a chance to get started."

No one was quick to write, some natural reluctance to "play along" inherent in the mix. About the four-minute mark, the scratch of pencil to pad was heard. Those who completed the task got more coffee or tea, as the rest wrote their selections.

Teo finally wrote three lines in a flowing cursive hand, his heart racing. Judy glanced at Teo's paper and raised an eyebrow. He just offered a little stiff smile and read his choices over again, nausea settling over him. What possessed him to choose these three?

"John Kirk?" Judy asked. "Would you go first?"

"Uh...sure." The big man squirmed a little and shared that he was named for the *Star Trek* character, and he'd hitchhiked across Europe after high school, but the group was unanimous in determining he'd never been a cheerleading squad leader. Judy's were equally diverse and entertaining— everyone wanted to see the belly dancing skills she'd learned at the community college.

Teo's fingers trembled as he waited for his turn. When it came, he read the sentences.

"I'm secretly in love with George Clooney.

"My life's ambition is to climb Mount Everest.

"I will be dead in less than one year."

First a hush, then uncomfortable laughter.

"Good one," Mitch said.

"He's never mentioned mountain climbing," Annike added, studying her officemate as if she could dissect him on the spot. "Though the Willis

Tower must be very attractive then."

Cattrin nodded. "Teodoro, why do you torment us so?" She pouted her lipsticked mouth.

Now that he'd said it, panic set in. He wished he could change what he'd written. It had been too much, too brave...too late. He forced a smile and fanned himself. "You all know how I feel about George."

After some more discussion and many teasing jabs, they voted that the death claim was the lie. Teo let them ease their minds with that choice, joining in their relieved laughter.

The dinner team left the room to cook a meal of roast beef and potatoes in a baking bag, setting up a salad and garlic bread on the side. Cattrin studied Teo as though he were some medical lab experiment.

"Perhaps there are always things you do not share with the rest of us, Teo," she said. She reached for the crumpled paper lying on the table.

Teo got it first. "Perhaps you don't know all that you think you do."

He turned his back on her and stared out the window, where gray-purple layered clouds moved in over the mountains. It would be evening soon. *More fun and games to come.* He didn't know if he'd be able to stand them.

* * * * *

CHAPTER 9

The truck rumbled on. After growled threats by the coyote, they'd fallen into an enforced silence as they crossed the border over an unmarked place. Inez understood the coyote had friends on the Border Patrol, friends who looked the other way late at night for a bit of the money.

It was a lot of money for him, but it was a lot of risk, too, if they got caught by the wrong people.

Half the money would go to Davi on the other end, who'd take them and drop them in the Mexican neighborhood in the city to make their way. He took the risk, too. The travelers only risked being deported to Mexico. The coyotes would go to jail.

The young woman next to her shifted in her sleep, her head falling on Inez' shoulder. She let it lie there. There was little enough comfort in this carton, this moving box rolling along the highway. The girl's hair smelled like that of Inez' sister Consuela.

The memory triggered by the scent brought a faint smile to her face. Consuela had been the pretty one, the popular one, when they'd been in school. She'd caught herself a fine man, who'd gone on to university at Mexico City, and was now an electrical engineer. They had a huge home, three cars and five healthy children. Consuela bragged about the parties she'd hold for people from her husband's office, the spreads of food, the flowers.

But with all Consuela had, she only managed to send a few hundred pesos to her mother every month. Her husband had other uses for the money, she said. She was sorry. Inez was left to care for their mother as best she could.

When she'd decided to take the chance for *El Norte*, she'd asked around to see how much money she would need for the crossing. She could have asked Consuela. But she knew what the answer would have been.

Finally she'd sold her small secondhand television, a couple of gold rings, and saved the rest from her meager earnings. She would ask no one.

Inez had never found a man who meant well. She was drawn to those with a streak of mischief and humor, often the type to let that mischief run free until it brought them to harm.After that red hot glow of lust, with laughing and warmth, good times and fast living, when she'd have her fun, her attraction inevitably faded. This time, she'd left a broken love affair with a married man who would never leave his wife for her.

It didn't seem fair. She was a good, moral person. She should have a good man.

Enough.

She wouldn't depend on a man to provide for her, or keep her warm, or even care for her. She held no delusions that she'd live a life of luxury in her new home—far from it. Illegal, working under the radar would be hard, no public benefits, only what she earned. She wouldn't have her own home, her own car, not until she saved for it.

But Inez had worked hard since she was ten years old. Her father had died and her mother had four children at home, two of them babies. Inez carried groceries for the local store, delivering them for a couple of pesos for the wealthy customers. She cleaned houses, watched children, scrubbed public bathrooms, whatever she could, to endure. And she didn't intend to stop now that she was bound for *El Norte*.

* * *

The box truck lurched from side to side as it ran over obstructions. Some of them had to be small boulders, from the way the truck tilted. Inez's neck wrenched until her eyes stung with tears.

They must be traveling through backcountry, avoiding *la migra* and the Border Patrol. Other than occasional shouted curses, quickly hushed, conversation among them died. Those who could move about a little to stretch tensed, weary muscles, but it was a hazardous choice.

Surely they'd been riding for hours. They had to be there soon.

Even the thought of Davi Pilar waiting for her didn't stop her from wishing that this leg of the journey would come to a swift end.

During one particularly rough shift, the bold young man who'd earlier caught her eye jumped up and jostled his way in half a space between her and the door. She had no choice but to scoot the sleeping girl from her shoulder and move aside to keep him from ending up in her lap.

"*Que pasa, nena?*" He snuggled close, apparently confident of his capability to win her. "*Me llamo Che Gomez. Y tu?*"

The introduction, under the circumstances, was so ridiculous, she smothered a laugh. This was no fancy *charro* dance, nor a *Quinceanera* to meet boys, or men for that matter. But the rest of the day had been so bleak, even this illusion of distraction was welcome.

Worse, Che was definitely her type, she thought with a sigh. That meant he was trouble. "Why should I give you my name, *muchacho*?"

"Because I could be the father of your children someday."

Che grinned, very white perfect teeth revealed in the faint light from the front. He was nice-looking, large, intelligent dark eyes, thick black hair trimmed neatly but not too short, a wide, friendly smile. While his body odor, like all the others, evidenced the strain of close quarters, he carried a trace of some aftershave that appealed to her.

His comment made her laugh aloud. "You are a cheeky monkey."

The truck rocked and knocked her into his shoulder. He slipped an arm behind to secure her, holding her close. "And you are a beautiful lady. Tell me your name."

She was glad he couldn't see her blush in the near-dark. She caught Rafael's faintly disapproving eye on her. Should she let him touch her? Of course not. He was a stranger. And up to no good, by the glint of mischief in his eyes.

But even this glimmer of choice, of free will, spurred her to do what she knew was wicked. "*Me llamo* Inez Suela. For all the good it will do you, *pappi*. In St. Louis we will find work and never see each other again."

"Ohhh. You are a pessimist, yes? The glass half empty. I see it as a chance to start over again in a new land, away from angry fathers with pregnant daughters." His voice was amused and definitely unrepentant.

"You made a girl pregnant and ran away?" She pushed him away. "Pig. No girl deserves to be treated in such a way."

Che laughed merrily. "See. You do like me."

She slapped him. "I don't like any man who could be so irresponsible!"

His eyes widened when she hit him, a dangerously hot fire blazing up in them. He stiffened and his hand came up, and just for a moment she wondered if it wasn't more than some pregnant girl that had forced him to leave Mexico. Would he hit her right in front of Rafael?

Control snapped into place at the last second, and finally he dropped his hand, forcing a grin. "Nonsense, *chica*. Why should I inflict someone as awful as myself on that poor girl for life? I'm giving her a gift beyond value."

Annoyed now, both at him and at herself for even entertaining a ghost of an idea that he might have been someone worth a relationship. "You are no gift," Inez muttered. "You are a pestilence."

She turned away from him and closed her eyes. "Go to sleep."

He only laughed softly. She leaned back, finding his arm still around her. Thinking of that poor abandoned girl, her instinctive rejection faded in the light of reality.

She was human, after all, and a woman with few comforts. Che's arm was softer—and warmer than the truck wall.

She turned away from him and tried to get some rest.

* * * * *

CHAPTER 10

Teo was first out of the room when Will announced a break. He ducked into the bathroom adjacent to his bedroom and leaned against the door, breathing hard. His heart fluttered in his chest like a panicked bird.

I almost did it.

I almost told them.

For five years, he'd kept secret that he was gay before he'd been forced out of the closet.

But to reveal he was HIV positive? Professional suicide.

He couldn't do it.

The struggle to conceal the truth grew harder each day, and now had become a nightmare. He'd hidden his AZT and the other cocktail drugs in that sock inside his case. But without his pager to remind him to take them on time, desperation clogged his veins until he was lightheaded.

If you don't take them on time, the virus could mutate. Again.

It hadn't been too long after he'd come out that a routine blood test cursed him with the diagnosis. He'd had no symptoms and few partners, so it had been easy to trace the culprit. Jose had been a professional man, a gallery owner and artist. Who would have suspected?

Not even Jose as it had turned out; he'd received his own diagnosis at nearly the same time. He'd apologized profusely to Teo, and of course he had been forgiven. It was just one of those things.

Some people got hit by a bus.

Some people got a slow, tortuous death sentence.

Once the shock receded, Teo educated himself on the best course of action. His doctors said general good health would go far toward keeping his T-cells up and avoiding the grip of opportunistic infections. He took handfuls of vitamins, watched his diet and exercise. His office mates teased him about the possibility of a new man. Why else would he be so careful?

A bad pneumonia the past November had shaken him like a dog tearing a chew toy, and his numbers plummeted. The doctors recommended he start the cocktail. He'd started as the sparkling ball fell in Times Square, sitting alone in his apartment, curtains pulled closed against the chilly Chicago winter winds. *Happy New Year, baby.*

The first month had been hell. But he forced himself to deal with the fatigue and the occasional nausea. He was almost used to it.

Since November, he'd been assured countless times that patients could remain HIV positive for years before developing full-blown AIDS, some as much as twenty years. He was fortunate in a way—he lived in one of the countries that treated HIV most aggressively, and he had access to clean water, nutritious food and medicines. As a black man in Africa, he'd probably have died months ago.

He tried to control his racing heart. *I can't believe I almost told them.* He didn't really anticipate dying in a year. He couldn't let himself think that way. But...it could be.

Teo washed his face with cold water, calmed himself with some deep breaths. It was still his secret. As long as no one searched his luggage, it remained his secret. Putting his usual smile on, he returned to the room, ready for the next round.

* * *

The coffee tray had been enhanced by the addition of several wine and beer bottles, for those who were ready to indulge. Teo chose another cup of green tea, pouring in water from a carafe on the counter, no sugar. He might allow himself a half glass of wine later, especially once he saw the recently-lauded Mommessin Beaujolais *nouveau*. An occasional indulgence was allowed despite his medications. And it was necessary for morale.

No one seemed to have noted his hurried exit or absence. Most of the lawyers were carefully not talking shop. Zanna flirted with John Kirk, her bright eyes flashing with excitement. A tinge of regret passed through him. Zanna was just the sort of girl his mother had wanted him to bring home— if things had been different. Leora Haroun was expansive and warm, her kitchen well stocked with homemade love in the form of baked goods and delicious casseroles. She'd accepted his life choices, though his father remained cold and distant to his death a few years ago.

Judy called them to dinner. The settings weren't of the sort that usually graced the retreat tables, with their multiple sparkling glasses and three sets of silverware. But the food looked tasty and there was plenty to go around, even with paper napkins and Corningware.

Teo ended between Mitch and Cattrin, not exactly his preference, but he made the effort to provide light repartee even though the extended day, travel included, had sucked the energy from him. Cattrin wouldn't let his earlier statement go, thickly veiled digs attempting to excavate the truth he'd hidden.

He should have known better. Of all the things, that would have been the one she'd focus on, like drops of blood in seawater to a tiger shark.

Cattrin's fluttering and chirping could seem harmless, her unabashed emulation of Annike and her social group. But Teo knew what she was capable of.

It had been the year the retreat took place at the Drake Hotel in Chicago, shortly before Mitch and Annike's separation. Teo had been very discreet, or so he'd thought, when his current flame happened upon them at the Palm Court. He'd taken Jacy aside, explained he was with the firm at an event, tried not to flinch at the acknowledgment of shame on his dear friend's face.

Cattrin's sharp eyes hadn't missed a thing. When he'd returned to the table where they were all having drinks, she'd invited him out onto the balcony overlooking the lake.

"He is a pretty boy, that one." She leaned on the polished rail, studying the night sky, where despite the city lights, they could still see stars. "He is special, *Teomino*?"

Teo's stomach roiled, threatened to spill the hundred-dollar meal he'd just consumed. "I've lived here for five years, Cattrin. It's logical to assume I'd make friends—"

"*Special* friends," she persisted, turning to study him like a specimen on a pin.

Trapped, he stared at her, knowing nothing he said would be right. He could argue, protest, but she'd take that as an admission. He'd seen it in her eyes, the knowledge that she "had" something on him. She'd been delighted. Wondering what payment she'd exact, a fleeting thought of suicide crossed his mind. But he was stronger than that.

He'd just smiled, leaving her in the lake-kissed breezes as he excused himself for the night.

In the morning, after very little sleep, he broke the news in a matter-of-fact way at breakfast. No one seemed terribly surprised; perhaps he hadn't been as discreet as he'd thought. Or maybe it just didn't matter. Cattrin looked crestfallen. Teo was pleased.

Just think what she'd do if she could get your latest secret into her hot little hands.

Judy interrupted Cattrin's prying intrusion. "So tell us, Cattrin, about your high school days. Spelling champion of the ninth grade?" She smiled warmly as she referred to one of the truths Cattrin had shared earlier.

The dark Filipino eyes danced with mischief. "I beat all the boys."

Mitch snorted. "Part of your bloodthirsty nature, no doubt."

Coming from Mitch, the comment was unexpected, and most of the people at the table raised an eyebrow.

Mitch grinned. "Well it's true. She's got an unerring sense of where she can hurt an opponent. She goes for that point till they yield. It's what I like about her."

"As long as she doesn't use that against her own team, that's a great talent," Will interjected gently.

After an awkward silence, Judy poured herself another glass of wine. "I know what I forgot to write down as one of my three. I was a member of the high school show corps. You know, those girls who march and wave the flags?" She laughed. "I haven't thought about that for a long time. Not that my legs are up to those short skirts anymore." She adjusted her glasses and lifted her glass with a rueful smile.

"None of ours are, honey," Teo assured her.

"Mine are." Cattrin puffed with pride. "Five hours of Pilates a week."

Judy shot a narrowed glance at Cattrin. "Ah. Well that's the difference. I spend that time driving the kids to soccer and sports events."

"We all have our priorities in life." Cattrin smirked, and then left the table.

The rest of them soon followed. The Harmonics team offered a final exercise for the evening, entitled *Marooned*, pooling ideas for survival on a desert island. The event was tense, despite Zanna's best efforts to cajole the lawyers into relaxation. When she suggested her first lifesaver would be Brad Pitt, the male lawyers laughed.

"Who needs that lightweight?" John Kirk interjected. "You're gonna play *Survivor*, you need a real man. Like Richard what's his name on the first season of the show. The naked guy."

"The tax evader?" Judy asked with a grin.

"Rather be naked with Brad, thanks," Zanna added.

Teo reinforced his earlier answer, taking the excuse to lighten the tension. "I'm telling you, George Clooney has him beat."

Each argued for their chosen necessities, and their combined years in the courtroom served them well. Not a one of them that couldn't make a dazzling argument at the drop of a hat.

Zanna chose the winners, not necessarily the team with the best tools, but the one that worked best together. Judy handed out thick envelopes, and the winners celebrated with another glass of wine.

Will finally relaxed, too, giving Zanna a wink. "Well done! As you probably guessed, the purpose of this exercise focuses on the teamwork, and how you gauge your co-workers' values by whether they pick a machete or...Brad Pitt. I think we can call it a success."

Annike waved her envelope with a catty smile. "At least I do."

Will laughed with her. "Well, ladies and gentlemen, that's all we have for now. Remember, if you want a GPS refresher, meet back here at seven."

The group broke up into small conversations. Noting it was time for his medicine, Teo slipped down the hall before the others and palmed his pills, then went for a drink of water in the bathroom. In secret agent mode, he entered one door and exited another, finding himself in the back corridor where the hot tub was located. Its cool blue tile was surrounded by potted plants of all kinds. Something to indulge with later. A beautiful setting like this was a precursor to serenity.

But first, a glass of Beaujolais nouveau awaited, with his name on it. He headed back to the kitchen, determined to shake his glum mood.

He couldn't let someone like Cattrin ruin what was left of his life. The days were precious now. He had to make them into what *he* wanted.

* * * * *

CHAPTER 11

Breakfast was served early in the morning, mindful of the GPS mini-workshop at seven. Teo arrived as the caretaker finished setting out the spread, assorted fresh fruit, containers of plain and fruited yogurt, bran cereal, bagels and muffins along with small jars of jelly and other condiments. "This looks delicious."

Jake Patrin grinned. "You're an early one. I think the rest haven't caught up to New Mexico time yet. Can I get you some coffee?"

"No, thanks. I'm a tea man." Teo poured hot water from a polished carafe over a green tea bag. "I'm from Chicago, so it's not so bad for me."

"Been there. Craziest drivers this side of New York City." Patrin chuckled, as he pointed a stocky remote control at the television and turned it on. He leaned against the counter, watching the weather forecast. "Damn."

Teo glanced at the screen. "That must be the snow you mentioned yesterday." As the perky Weather Channel forecaster advanced the maps through the week, he could see indications were for upward of a foot of snow. "Is that usual?"

Patrin shook his head. "Not usual by this time of year, but not unheard of. Looks to be the worst in twenty years, though."

Teo crossed to the picture window where they'd watched a spectacular sunset the night before. From the east, behind the house, the sun was just adding a patina of orange to the sands that stretched toward the mountains as far as he could see.

"The *casa* seems to be built fairly strong. We'll be fine, right?"

"Oh sure. We been through a lot worse. You all don't need to worry a bit—just get your outdoor stuff done next couple of days. But I still have some hatches to batten. Have a good one, friend." Patrin drained his coffee and left the kitchen through a back hallway.

Curious, Teo followed Patrin's footsteps, just long enough to see where the corridor led. A mudroom with hooks for coats and a tray full of grimy boots waited at its other end, and past there, a door to a graveled path leading to a large garage. Patrin disappeared into it, then came out with a handful of tools and rode away on a small tractor.

Sounds of habitation issued from the kitchen, and Teo returned there, finding Mitch with a coffee cup in hand, looking as though he hadn't slept much. "Ready for the day's events?"

The senior partner's voice resonated with a lack of enthusiasm. "I figured I'd better be able to lead the charge on this treasure hunt thing."

Teo smiled, knowing Mitch's love of gadgetry. "You're an outdoorsman, though. And a technophile. It'll be second nature."

Smearing cream cheese thickly on an onion bagel, Mitch grumbled. "Rather be skiing."

"You might be able to, come the end of the week." Teo explained the forecast they'd seen.

Mitch brightened. "The week won't be a total loss then." He picked up the remote, changing the channel to ESPN for the basketball news.

Maybe that bottle of merlot Mitch emptied last night had something to do with his dreary outlook. Or was it the tension that still remained in the air?

The edgy atmosphere after dinner had mellowed somewhat with the shared consumption of several bottles of the excellent wine. John Kirk monopolized young Zanna, while her partner never objected. Instead, Will spent the evening curled up in a chair by the stone fireplace with a James Patterson book.

Teo surmised they must not be a couple.

The attorneys clumped together in the conversation pit, chatting over personal matters. Judy had signed a contract on a new condo at Vallagio Inverness, now that she was on her own with her two sons. Cattrin planned a trip to Indonesia to visit ailing grandparents.

Annike brought up the idea of co-authoring a book on one of their more successful clients, and Mitch encouraged her.

"You know you've always wanted to write, Annie. You're good at it."

Languid, the blonde waved her stemmed glass. "I don't know, Mitch, it would take so much time from the other work. I do need to have a social life, you know. *You* do." The spiteful smirk on her face was mirrored on Cattrin's, both thriving on conflict like emotional fertilizer.

And that's my cue.

Teo finished his ruby Beaujolais, bid them goodnight and took his glass to the kitchen, Cattrin's gaze burning after him. He didn't know how late they'd all gone to bed; his exhaustion let him sleep through any noise they'd made when they came in.

"Georgetown better get on the stick."

Mitch's comment dragged Teo's attention back to the present. He didn't follow sports generally, though he was a great fan of the underdog Chicago Cubs, just as a matter of principle and civic pride. Before he could reply, Mitch moved on.

"You're a skier, aren't you, Teo? Taos isn't but an hour drive. Pretty country. I really wasn't expecting the chance to hit the slopes, but I'm thinking that would be one hell of a bonus."

"It certainly would."

Teo wasn't convinced he would actually ski, if the opportunity presented itself. Keeping his energy level up was a prime focus, especially with Cattrin ready to pick him apart at the earliest opening. "I suppose if we get everything done that Judy's got in mind…"

"Better than slogging through a case debrief, which is what Annie will want to do, I'm sure. She's always nagging me about interoffice memos."

Teo sipped his tea. He'd be perfectly happy with a couple hours in the chair by the fireplace, some jazz on the stereo system, and a chance to just let his mind lie fallow.

But that's not likely in this crowd.

"I'm sure there will be time for both."

"From your lips to God's ears, my friend." Mitch chuckled and finished his bagel, using the creamy side to dab up bits of crunchy onion that had fallen off.

Judy's sharp laugh came from the door. "I didn't know you were a religious man, Mitch." She came in, stopping at the counter to survey the choices.

"No atheists in a foxhole." Mitch smirked and drank his coffee fast.

Judy looked to Teo. "What are we petitioning God for now?"

"What our plans might be later in the week."

She turned her attention to Mitch. "I'd expected to work with the Harmony team as long as possible. If we have meetings after that—"

"Only the Lotus-Eaters could really last a whole week without responsibilities. I promised you we'd get through whatever hoops you have planned. We can brainstorm about hang-ups and clients Thursday or Friday, I guess." He gave her a brief update on the weather situation. "So we'll play your games before that settles in, and then stay indoors and see what happens."

"Or bail for Taos to ski," Teo added with a wink.

Judy made a face. "It's March, for heaven's sake. Spring! How bad could the snow get?" She searched through the box of assorted tea bags, coming up with a packet of chai tea.

"That's not my department." Mitch stretched, then got up for more coffee. "Entertainment is in your purview."

The noise level doubled in a matter of seconds with the entrance of Will and Zanna, John Kirk hot on their heels, chatting companionably with the petite blonde.

"So these are the brave explorers," Will said with a smile. "Let me grab a muffin and we can get started." He counted the people. "Missing a few."

"Their loss," Teo said firmly as he joined Judy and Mitch.

"Maybe they know how to use the equipment already," Zanna suggested.

"Ha!" Mitch quipped. "The only equipment Annie knows how to use is a hair dryer and a Mastercard."

Amid the ensuing laughter, Zanna handed out plastic containers the size of shoeboxes to each person. Will climbed onto a table in the front of the room, sitting Indian-style facing them, wolfing down his food.

Teo opened his box and leafed through the contents, a map with concentric lines, some brightly colored plastic coins, a compass, a couple of pencils and markers, and a device about the size of a large cell phone.

The others did the same.

Finally Mitch held up a pencil. "I know how to use this."

That made everyone laugh. Will applauded. "Hey, that's a start. All right, what you've got in there are some topographical maps and two devices to help you navigate. The compass, I'm sure you know. The other is a GPS. You know what that means?"

John Kirk grabbed a banana from the counter. "Geo Positioning something."

"Global Positioning System," Will corrected. "Once you connect with at least three satellites, the GPS can tell you where you are on the earth. We're lucky out here, because there aren't buildings or canyon walls to block off the signals."

"So what is this? One of those Army exercises where you drive us forty miles out in the desert and we have to find our way home?" Mitch's brow furrowed with concern.

"Not at all," Will said, with a patient-like-dealing-with-young-children tone. "Actually, after we're finished here, Zanna and I are going to plant your caches. If you'll look on page one of the materials, you'll see what I'm talking about.

"Today's geo-teaming exercise will be an easy one, till we're sure everyone can use the GPS. The point will be to find three different boxes we've hidden around the property. They'll be in an ammo case like this." He held up a gray metal box about a foot long and six inches across. "And you'll have the coordinates of exactly where it's placed."

John Kirk scratched his head. "So you're going to go put it there and tell us where it is, and we just have to haul ourselves out there and pick it up and bring it back."

Zanna paused in her loading of the boxes. "It's not exactly that easy. The GPS will tell you where it is. That's like me telling you a cache is in— oh, the Empire State building. The GPS will have the coordinates for the building, but that really doesn't solve the problem for you. You'll have to make some other decisions to figure out exactly where it is."

"Right. And don't move it. You'll sign the book in the cache, leave one of your coins there, and then come back, after you've found all three. Tomorrow there will be five." Will checked his notes. "Your team can divide up the tasks. Someone can hold the maps, someone can manage the GPS, and so on."

"This isn't like any map I've ever seen." Teo leaned back in his chair.

"These maps help with the Empire State problem," Zanna said, walking over to their table to spread out the map. "It's a topographical map, the height of the ground. The GPS can get you to the foot of El Capitan, but unless you know from your map the box is 3,000 feet straight up, you'll be hard pressed to find it."

As the lesson progressed, even those most determined to resist became fascinated. Judy and John Kirk had used the handhelds before, so they helped some of the less tech savvy members of the group. Annike and Cattrin entered fashionably late but at least became enamored with the idea of competition.

When they'd finished eating, the group moved outside to practice triangulating their position and orienting themselves with compasses. The trainers left, both sporting heavy-duty backpacks.

Judy pulled the back sheet off the packet. "Here's the directions, folks. Each team should find all three caches, then report back here. Will says something in each cache gives a clue about the other two."

Faced with a treasure hunt, Teo felt like a kid again. His mother often arranged scavenger hunts for the neighborhood children, sending them cruising the surrounding blocks for assorted obscure objects, escapades he remembered from childhood with much pleasure. *This will be fun. No matter whether I find the boxes or not.*

When Will and Zanna returned forty-five minutes later, they took each of the GPS units and programmed sets of coordinates into it.

"All right," Will said. "You're in business. You should form teams. We've got five GPS units, so you can do twos, threes, whichever you want.

What do you think, Judy? Mix up the offices again? Or leave this one to chance?"

She smiled with mock magnanimity. "Let's give them a break. Choose your own teams."

"We'll go with Gianni." Cattrin stepped over to the Denver partner and took his arm, smiling up at him seductively. "Annie-ka and I can use the help."

Annike glanced a moment at Mitch, then sidled over to the younger man in agreement. "Experience does count."

Teo picked up a GPS from the table. "I'm ready. Anyone brave enough to go stumble around the sage with me? Judy?"

"I'm exercising pre-emptive senior partner authority," Mitch said. "Judy goes with me. That way I don't get lost."

"You come too, Teo," Judy said with a grin. "Save me!" she added in a stage whisper.

Mitch eyed Teo and set his empty coffee cup on the counter. "Please tell me you're a closet Master Hiker."

"No, no, I'm out of the closet these days." Teo winked and smiled. "It's all adventure now."

"Great. We are *so* dead." Mitch groaned and slipped on a Land's End sweatshirt, tugged the hem down. "Let's do it."

Will Starlin gathered the extra equipment and tucked it in his pack. "Zanna and I have walkie-talkies, and we'll be in the field. There's only 500 acres here, and it's fenced along the outside. We marked the compound on your map. Keep track of your direction, so you can at least get back to the house, if you can't find the caches. There's a mirror in your kit, to signal if you can't get yourself home."

"Signal? You mean Morse code?" Mitch looked at the mirror Judy held.

"No, not at all." Will laughed. "Just hold the mirror up in the sunlight and tilt it back and forth. It'll catch someone's eye. Mr. Patrin said he'd be watching too. We gave him our walkie-talkie frequency, and he's got binoculars."

The lawyers filed toward the door, activating the small screens on the GPS units and getting bearings. Mitch sucked in a large breath. "All right, troops. Let's take San Juan Hill!"

* * * * *

CHAPTER 12

Davi Pilar checked his truck and slammed the back door closed. Everything was ready.

Sitting on the concrete step outside the building where he rented a two-room flat, he scanned up and down the street. Couldn't be too careful. It's why he had put the holes in the top of his box truck, instead of the front or sides. His *pollos* could get the air they needed and the casual passerby wouldn't wonder why the truck had been altered. He didn't want to lose the lifestyle he had coming to him, not for carelessness.

The neighborhood didn't look like much. Kids without shoes or coats played with battered Tonka trucks on the sidewalks, scraggly grass all that grew in the few patches of dirt between the concrete. The women would plant flowers, come summer, try to decorate the place, but it was still what it was—a rundown ethnic ghetto.

Inside, though, that was another story.

Davi might only have two rooms, but he had three times the possessions he'd ever owned in Juarez, and better ones. He had a full-size refrigerator that dispensed cold water and ice from the door. He owned a top-flight stereo and huge speakers. His bed pillow was of polyester instead of old feathers, and his bedspread looked like black and red satin. He bought good whiskey, nothing smuggled any more, and top-name commercial tequila, much better than what his cousin used to bring in from the backlands.

The next scheduled acquisition on his list was a big-screen television, big like a movie screen. None of his family had ever had a big-screen television. He'd get hi-def, be able to watch the football games better than anyone. Once he scored this drop, he'd have the money.

The night before, Tonio's brother Juan called to let Davi know the truck was on its way to New Mexico. It was time for Davi's part. Tonio's fat *hermano* promised that Tonio had Davi's money, that it had been a good crop of human cargo, the truck full of those bound for *El Norte*.

"You'd better not be lying to me," Davi growled. "If I don't get my money, and my people, I'll come down there and—"

"Davi, Davi! Calm yourself!" Juan assured him all would be well.

"Besides, you'll be surprised who's coming to meet you."

"I don't like surprises."

"You'll like this one." There was a dark little amusement in the man's tone that angered Davi. "An old friend of yours."

"Who? Who is it?" Davi kicked the leg of his heavy sofa in his agitation, muttering curses as the pain shot through his foot and leg.

"You'll see, *compadre*. Maria needs me now. Meet them tomorrow night. *Hasta la luego!*" The line went dead.

Bastardo.

Davi brooded about that cryptic warning even now, sitting on the step. Who might be coming? One of the men he'd crossed before he'd left town? The husband of his sister, who had threatened him after Davi had taken her small savings? He'd burned a lot of bridges when he'd left Mexico for the North. It could be anyone.

When he left later that night, he took two handguns and a rifle. Just in case.

* * * * *

CHAPTER 13

An hour after they'd begun, they were ready to quit. Judy had blisters, Mitch had stopped talking at all and even Teo found himself snapping—and they hadn't found one cache.

They'd walked several miles. He was sure of it. The landscape so appealing from the window with its varied rainbow tones was unremarkably the same in person, yard after yard of reddish dirt and sand with scrubby vegetation sticking out every so often. The dry wind had picked up with a hint of chill, sending dust into their faces. If it hadn't been for the small metal compass in his hand, they'd have gone in circles. *Hopeless.*

"What have we got, fifty years of education among us?" Judy complained. "How can we not find it?"

Teo pulled his sheet with directions from his sweatshirt's front pouch and read it over again, frowning as another team's cry of victory farther west carried to them on the wind. "We're right here, where the coordinates say," he said thoughtfully. "We've cross-checked, we've verified the data. But there's not a box that size anywhere! We've been over this same twenty square feet half a dozen times."

Mitch grimaced, sitting on a large rock. He rubbed his scalp as if it would stimulate his brain. "Then it's just more obvious. It's got to be the Empire State Building."

"What?" Teo frowned, confused.

"Remember what the girl said? We've got a twenty-foot radius, but just because you're on the spot..." Mitch took the GPS to the coordinate center. "Now. The Empire State Building goes up and down."

Teo studied the landscape for a hint, but it was very flat. *Not much to choose from.* There were a few low piñons nearby, and he looked in their branches and gingerly felt the trunk for a possible false front. "Not up."

"Down?" Judy raised an eyebrow and looked around her feet. "We did this. It wasn't—" Teo looked at her with dawning realization. "That rock Mitch was sitting on."

She nodded, excitement growing, and raced him back to it. Sure enough, the box was in a hollow under the rock nearly hidden behind several other smaller chunks of tawny stone.

"Yes!"

Teo picked her up in a hug, sweeping her off her feet. "You did it!"

"We did it," she corrected with a grin.

They were so relieved they were not total failures, they nearly forgot to leave the coin token from their pack as they had been instructed. In the log, Mitch read that the other team had already found this cache. "Figures," he complained.

Teo grinned, good spirits restored, and finished their brief written entry with a quick sketched rendition of a hawk in flight before he replaced the case.

Judy insisted on celebration, so they broke out bottled water. At that moment, it tasted as delicious as any champagne Teo had ever had.

Rejuvenated, they continued to the next point, a little wiser and more prepared. They found the second cache inside a saguaro cactus, removing it with great care though they gained several bloody fingers. The other team had already found that one, apparently by the same method, as red-brown fingerprints dotted the log book. A nearly unintelligible note with some hostile curse words was made in John Kirk's sharp slanted hand, making Judy smile.

The third cache was tucked behind a metal fence post by the barn, just out of sight. It was the closest to the *casa* and would have been the easiest, if the team had been a little more experienced.

Walking up the stone driveway to the casa, Teo waved as Will Starlin came out of the garage, his cheeks flushed with the morning's activity.

"How'd you like it?" Will asked. "Find everything?"

"Great," Judy replied.

Mitch grunted and walked inside. "Just great."

Will frowned at the blood on Judy's hands. "Better go wash that. We didn't think that cache would dig itself so far in the cactus. Sorry."

She nodded and followed Mitch inside, Teo right after her as Will greeted the other team.

Cold cuts and cheeses with assorted breads and condiments were laid out on the counter when he returned to the main area. Cattrin and Annike pulled bags of flavored chips and heavy-duty red paper plates from the storage cupboard. Mitch went for the Heineken. "Anyone else?"

"That all we got?" John Kirk frowned as he peeled off his navy sweatshirt, showing a ripple of taut stomach muscle under his soft jersey shirt. "Regular beer is like soda pop."

"Don't worry, your Guinness is in there. How you can drink it, I have no clue. That black stuff is nasty." Judy set a bottle on the counter. "Everyone come help themselves."

Sheepish but proud, John Kirk reached for the bottle and took a long drink. "Mmmm. Can't help it. I acquired the habit when I spent a year at Oxford. The family I rented from practically lived at the pub down the block." He shrugged and handed Zanna another of the dark brews as she slipped up behind him with a coquettish smile.

"Oh, Gianni, I love Europe!" Cattrin said as she balanced a few tomato slices on a lettuce leaf. "Especially Italy. Ah, la Firenze, la Roma, shopping on the piazza of Torino..." She sighed dramatically.

"Well, I don't know about all that," John Kirk said, brow furrowed. "But I liked the pubs. Whole families go, and spend a whole evening there. Great community place. Made a lot of good friends that way." He gave a mock woeful look at his bottle. "Killed a lot of these, too."

His smirk made Cattrin roll her eyes and she took her tiny salad away to eat it with the barest spritz of lemon. The men monopolized the counter, competing to see who could make the manliest Dagwood, piling ingredients onto hearty brown bread.

Mitch looked up from his creation, pitched his voice to carry. "I see our trainers in the back there—are we booked up this afternoon?"

Will shook his head. "Not unless you want more practice with the GPS. We'd expected you'd have a more difficult time. You guys is smart!" He grinned.

"Well, gee thanks." Mitch's tone bore the undercurrent of friendly sarcasm. "We do try. Anyway, in light of some free time and a message left by the Chicago office, I'd like to pull together a meeting at about two." He held up a sandwich that had to be four inches thick. "Bon appetit."

With a two-hour reprieve, Teo made a sandwich of turkey and swiss on ciabatta bread, skipping the chips for a peach left from breakfast. He took his lunch to the window seat, where he sat comfortably alone, watching carrion birds fly in the distance as the gray clouds built up.

* * * * *

CHAPTER 14

Inez woke when Rafael Diego kicked her foot. Asleep, Che's head rested on the wall, his arm still around her shoulder.

"What is it?" she asked softly.

"It is taking too long."

Inez shrugged. "How can you tell? It's so dark." She studied her shadowed companions, many of them snoring.

He tapped his watch and its face lit up, a ghostly half-light shining on his face.

"Ah. Perhaps they had to take a detour to avoid *la migra*."

"Perhaps."

They were silent for several minutes, taking in the complaints and murmurs of the others, the rumbling of the truck engine and the jerking of the bed caused by poor suspension. The road was rough, perhaps even rougher than earlier. Inez thought it must be a dirt road, maybe a dried-up river bed with rocks, something.

Could they be lost?

What would happen if they didn't meet the driver for the next leg of the journey?

A pale sickness washed through her at the thought of having to return home in defeat. She'd taken everything she had, all her money, all her courage, and screwed it to the wall for this one opportunity. She didn't know if she'd be tough enough to do it a second time.

"*Que pasa?*" the young man beside her mumbled.

"We still aren't there." Rafael eyed Che with disapproval. "You shouldn't bother her."

Inez raised an eyebrow. "He's not bothering me."

"Yeah, old man, I'm not bothering her. See?" White teeth gleamed in the half-darkness. "She likes me."

"I do not." Inez eyed him. "You are a pig."

"What?" Che cried in mock disappointment. "How could you not? I am pretty. I am polite. I am *muy macho*." He posed and smirked at her.

"I don't care if you're the biggest stud in Mexico, I don't have to like you. There is more to being a man than having a *masacuata*." She poked him in the groin. "If you are man enough to make someone pregnant, you should be man enough to stay and be father to the child as well."

Che pulled back and she thought he would hit her, but his hands dropped to his side.

"Father? And what is so great about being a father, huh? My father, he see I look like my Mestizo *madre*, he take a focking walk! He goes north, comes home every couple years with a new car and a gold necklace for his new *puta*, shows the world what a real man he is, huh?" He got louder. "You think he give my mama a penny of all this money? You think he give anything for me and my brother? Hell no!"

Up on his knees, he slammed a fist into the side of the truck. The metal reverberated all the way to the front, sparking a rabble of conversations.

Rafael tried to shut the boy up, but this was clearly an argument Che had played out in his head a thousand times. Inez felt like it would have to roll to its conclusion. She looked away, embarrassed for the young man.

"So I finally get a chance to meet him, this big *hombre*, my 'father'." He said the word as if it burned his throat like a raw ancho chile. "I see him in a bar at Christmas, spending money like water, buying drinks for everyone, and he see me. He says, 'Oh look here, it's an Indian boy. Wait—I slept with his mother!' He laughs and his friends laugh. I walk over to him and he looks me in the eye. He say, 'You are nothing. You will never be anything. *Pinche* Mestizo.'

"So I think a minute, then I swing a fist into his gut and when he bends over, I kick my knee into his nose and break it. I take a roll of bills from his pocket for my mother. I swore in front of all those people that I would be something. I would have the same flashy car and wad of money that that man had—better! Better!"

Che glared at everyone who stared at his outburst. No one said a word.

"So I'm going to America. And I'll have it. Please forgive me*, senorita*, if you think I don't know what it takes to be a father. I never had one." Sulking, he leaned back against the wall and pulled his hat low over his eyes, ending the conversation.

Inez exchanged curious looks with Rafael. He frowned and shook his head, made a gesture for her to come sit next to him. She thought about it a moment, then felt a little smile creep to her lips. She actually liked Che better now that he'd made his confession.

Her heart was in real trouble. She leaned back next to him and closed her eyes again, praying for their safe and quick arrival.

* * * * *

CHAPTER 15

The next morning, as he set out what seemed to be enough food to feed a small village in Central America, Jake Patrin considered his guests. Though he hadn't really "spied" on them, it was his responsibility to make sure they had what they needed, so he kept close, often listening from the next room or watching them outside.

He'd played his usual mystery guessing game, stereotyped them from the beginning. There were the prissy ladies, the guy a little light in the loafers, the aging jock who still considered himself a big stud. The little Asian one always followed the older blonde with envious eyes.

The boss man? One of those born to money who wanted to be appreciated for his mature good looks and wealth, so he surrounded himself with fawning employees.

Judy, now she was down to earth. He could understand her. *One out of six ain't bad.*

Then the younger crew, a working team, fueled by youthful enthusiasm and—what? The girl. The little cheerleader type, she seemed a bit over the top. His radar pinged about her. Something was a little shonky, as his old Aussie mate T-Bone would have said, her eyes over-bright, her energy too nervous.

He couldn't put his finger on it. But there was something.

This visit had an air of unreality. Some groups renting the ranch had spiritual retreats, an escape from the modern technological world. They had him remove the big-screen tv, the videos. They came to get away.

This group seemed to have brought most of the whole mess with them.

This spread had to set them back a hundred, maybe a hundred and a quarter, breakfast for eight people. *Well, nine, if you count me...and Judy said I could help myself.* Gourmet coffee, organic fruit, the best of everything.

These guys must make a mint.

He'd seen the receipt that had come with the supplies when they'd been delivered the week before. Four grand, including the alcohol, everything they could want for a week from fruit to nuts. Like he said, enough for a whole village in a third world country, more most likely.

His impressions of the group were just that, of course. Impressions.

No one was ever what they seemed on the surface, and no doubt some had depths he didn't suspect. All the same, he'd overheard a couple of them talking wistfully about their cell phones, which they'd apparently left in a locker at the airport. Seemed like a waste to him. Point of that phone was to take it wherever you were. He shrugged.

City folk.

At least no one had complained about the facilities yet, no matter how much they may have looked down their noses at it when they arrived. He'd suspected they'd have nothing to grumble about. Jake took his caretaker responsibilities seriously.

Which reminds me, I've still got to put the last touches on that window...

Finished with the breakfast trays, he took a thick ceramic mug and filled it with coffee. It tasted better than anything he'd ever had at the ranch, but it was Jamaican Blue Mountain coffee—at fifteen dollars a pound, he'd expect it to be delicious. Maybe even do magic tricks.

He carried the cup and a plain bagel into the rec room and used the remote to activate the TV, tuning in the Weather Channel. Some perky brunette blithely described the warm sunny spring in Atlanta, where the studio was based, wide smile on her face.

"Yeah, yeah, get to the bad news," he grumbled. He sat on the arm of a brown leather chair, letting coffee chase the chill that had set into his bones earlier when he'd walked the perimeter.

Soon enough, the tag-teamed male meteorologist moved with the map to the western half of the country, where ominous clumps of green, pink and white covered New Mexico. In their corner, it was mostly white. When it switched to numbers, Tres Piedras was designated as "twelve plus" inches. The announcer confirmed that near the mountains, it could be much more.

"Sometime tonight. Wonderful." Jake finished his coffee, thinking of all the outside chores he'd have to take care of before the snow hit. Seemed like his guests would have most of the day to wrap up the outdoor activities, but then they'd be inside for several more.

Not like they didn't have enough alcohol to keep their toesies warm.

His mouth dried up, considering what awaited in the closet just feet from where he stood.

With that thought driving him, Jake headed out to the barn to make sure everything was buckled down. Anything to escape that temptation for just a minute, long enough for it to pass.

* * *

Later in the morning, the teams set out for the open again, armed with maps and handhelds, dressed a little warmer today as the winds had picked up over the mountains from the north. He shook his head, letting his thick coffee cup warm his hands.

Why city folk would pay all this money to come wander around the scrub looking for ammo boxes wasn't his to question, really. People could spend their money on lots of stupid things. *Like the cases of beer and wine in the pantry.*

He wished he could quit thinking about those. Just knowing they were there was hard. He'd liked a good shot of Southern Comfort back in the day. But he'd given up alcohol along with drugs as a matter of principle.

His sponsor had suggested the idea when Jake had first joined the Narcotics Anonymous group in King City. Jake had been tempted to substitute a little brain-fogging whiskey for the Oxycontin, but his sponsor made it very clear that wouldn't solve the problem.

Best he'd learn to cope cold sober, that was the plan.

A hard one, but it had worked. Thirteen months of sobriety. He had the red, blue, yellow and moonglow NA keytags, one celebrating each three months so far. He hoped to earn many more, get that black one on his chain.

But there was an awful lot of booze in that pantry.

Jake lit a cigarette, grateful he still allowed himself that vice. The action bought him some private time to stop, relax, ponder the inequities and blessings of the universe, then fill his lungs with fresh air when he'd finished.

Back in the *casa*, he took a soft brush mop to the floors in all the common areas. With the doors and windows shut against the cool breeze, there wasn't much dust, but he maintained the *casa* every day, guests or not. It was part of the routine. The routine kept him on the path, kept him from thinking about things he shouldn't.

Mostly.

When he'd finished his rounds, he took to the outdoors to clear his head. He spotted a flash of light, then another and another, from the northwest quadrant of the ranch. Someone was signaling with their mirror. He pulled the walkie-talkie from his belt and called the training team.

"What's up?" the young man answered, sounding out of breath.

"You got someone blinking about halfway out to the northwest fence post," Jake said. "Don't have the binoculars, or I'd tell you who. Got my suspicions, though." He chuckled, remembering the kind of shoes he'd seen on some of the women that morning.

"Thanks, Mr. Patrin. We'll head out there now."

"Let me know if you need help. I've got a little tractor to drive out if you need it."

His eye caught movement in the field to his right as the two took off at a run from the midpoint of the arroyo in the direction of the mirror. Curious, he stepped back inside for the binoculars and climbed up on the picnic table bench to watch. They were still too far away to identify, but the two met up with several other people. There was a lot of bobbing and weaving before the walkie-talkie crackled to life again.

"Mr. Patrin? Can you bring that tractor?" Starlin's tone was troubled but not urgent. "We'll need to transport someone back in."

"Sure thing, son. Be right out."

Jake headed for the barn and took the keys off the hook inside the door, firing up the John Deere. It was a 5105 utility model, heavy enough to pull the wagon fully loaded with cut wood. He hauled the wagon over, tossed the first aid kit into it, then went to meet them.

As he pulled through a clump of scrub some fifteen minutes later, he found half a dozen of the guests clustered in two groups, one gathered around the broad-shouldered younger man from Denver and the other staring pointedly at something on the ground. Jake parked the tractor next to the man with his leg propped up on a rock. "What happened?"

"It bit him. He could die!" the tall blonde said, pointing to the other group. Jake saw a brown and white banded snake lying on the ground near them, unmoving, oddly twisted.

"He's *not* going to die." The cheerleader's tone sounded like it was about the hundredth time she'd made the statement.

Jake walked over and peered at the snake. A year as an Army medic in the jungles of Central America taught him a lot—the tropics grew all kinds of fauna that did not take kindly to humans invading their space. He brought the first aid kit over to check the man's leg, bleeding from a couple of puncture wounds mid-shin. "King snake," he said. "Not poisonous. We'll haul him back to the *casa*, get some ice on it, he should be fine by morning."

John Kirk seemed to droop with relief. "That's good news."

"Told you." The little blonde's tone held a taut undercurrent.

"Fortunately, we'd about wrapped up the main exercise." Will pulled his light parka a little closer in the wind, now flecked with occasional snowflakes. The sky to the northwest was heavy, laden with thick foamy gray clouds which promised every inch of the forecast blizzard. "Did you all exchange information? How could you have found four that fast?"

Mitch grinned. "Teamwork. That's why we're here, isn't it?"

Jake and Teo helped John Kirk onto the wagon, Zanna crawling on beside him to "brace the bandage."

Jake smirked. *Little girl…you're looking to find you a sugar daddy? And then what?*

He still wondered about her, that almost electric buzz that ran in her. Maybe young women were just different these days, what with their celebrity role models. But if he'd had a daughter, he'd have much preferred her to grow up like Mary Ann than Ginger. "Hold on back there, soldier, it's a rough ride."

It took nearly twenty minutes back to the main house, because of detours required by the terrain. The tractor was heavy-duty, but the ground was uneven and the wagon jerked from side to side. The others made it back fifteen minutes later, on foot. By then, John Kirk was ensconced in a padded chair in front of the wide-screen TV, his leg disinfected, iced and propped up, Zanna tending to his every need as he caught up with the latest sports scores.

Jake helped Judy pull out the trays for lunch, though it was half an hour before schedule. "Looks like it's about time to buckle down and stay in, ma'am," he said.

She sighed. "I think you're right. At least we made it back in one piece." She glanced over to John Kirk, who seemed delighted at the attention he was getting. "Most of us, anyway."

Jake kept to himself his earlier suspicions about the injured parties. God had a way of surprising him every day. "You want this soup out?"

"Soup sounds great. Thanks."

The caretaker rooted through the second refrigerator and brought out a container of minestrone, setting it on the stove to heat.

"That looks like everything. If you don't need me, I should lock down before the storm."

"Sure, we can handle this. Thanks for the rescue."

"No problem, ma'am. We aim to please." Jake grinned and forced himself past the pantry, and its contents, heading out to put the tractor away. He eyed the darkening skies. *Hope these folks have plenty to do the next several days. It's gonna be a whopper.*

* * * * *

CHAPTER 16

Davi Pilar sped along Interstate 44 late on Tuesday night, his focus a rendezvous with the truck coming from Taos. He knew he had to turn west on Highway 412 after he got to Tulsa. Dark eyes searched the roadside for the marker.

Sounded easier than it was at the moment.

Freakish storm was setting in over the Southwest, and he was scheduled to drive right into it. He was running behind because of the blowing snow and wind, and the crazy *gringos* who didn't know how to drive in snow.

The *desmadre* trail. Total chaos.

Davi stepped harder on the accelerator, sliding slightly as he passed a green Chevy, shivering despite the fan straining to chunk bits of heat out of the dash.

Old Tonio, he could make this run easy from Mexico, fat man in that old brown parka, he'd be warm. But not Davi. He was always in motion, burning up his energy, freezing out here on the damned road. But he had good reason.

He honked his horn as he passed the Chevy, the routine a mantra in his head, staving off the cold and the loneliness for a few minutes. *No time for you, old man. I got ten thousand dollars waiting for me at that rest stop. Pick up a load of pollos middle of the night, put em in the truck and carry them to St. Louis.*

All there was to it. Tonio would meet him, pay him and he'd be on his way home a rich man.

If he ever got past the damn snow. He turned on the radio, listened desperately for a weather forecast. Blizzard warnings dominated all the channels, warning people to stay off the roads, and have their tire chains ready if they had to drive in the mountains.

"Jesus!" Davi growled and flipped the windshield wipers to high as the snow came down more heavily.

Just two more days, one there and one back. That's all. Was it so much to ask?

He plowed on through the snowstorm as though the devil drove him. His stomach filled with acid as he fell farther and farther behind schedule.

He bet the devil he'd get there.

And Tonio had better be waiting with his cargo of forty. He'd better. Or else.

* * * * *

CHAPTER 17

Something was wrong. Really wrong.

The unevenness of the ride for the last hour had kept Inez from sleep, and judging by the worried whispers of her companions, she wasn't the only one. The truck slid on the road surface a few times and bumped along. Clearly, the driver was having trouble.

Rafael lit his tiny flashlight briefly, shone it over the group. "Calm down, my friends. My watch tells me we have now traveled enough time— we will meet our driver soon." His voice was soft but authoritative. He nodded to Inez.

She nodded back.

A buzz of chatter followed, but it slowly subsided.

Che Gomez leaned on the wall, hunched over, his gaze seeking hers in the faint light. Could he be frightened? She wondered, unable to read the emotion in his eyes. She certainly was.

The ride came with a certain amount of risk. She knew that. She also knew she was in control of nothing at this point. She was merely locked in the back of a dark metal truck.

Perhaps the driver was still on that back road. Maybe he was eluding the U.S. border officials by traveling through an arroyo, the wet mud causing the truck's tires to lose traction. The coyote could even be urging him to do it just for the fun of scaring his cargo.

Anything was possible.

She reached out for the side of the truck, found it very cold. Could it be snow? Her experience was limited, though she knew ice and snow could cause a vehicle to slide in this manner. But this was a heavy truck. How much snow would it take to affect its course? That she didn't know.

Inez caught Che's look again, and forced a smile. "A macho man like you, worried about some noise? Come now."

"I wouldn't worry if I were the one driving," he said with a hostile undercurrent.

"I can understand." She grabbed at him as the truck slid again, this time a considerable distance before it righted its path.

"But it's nice to be close to you," he whispered softly as Rafael turned off his light. He moved close to her, closer than she intended, and she tried to re-create a comfortable space under Rafael's watchful eye. Though she wouldn't have minded some comfort at that moment.

"Like I said, when we get to St. Louis—"

She never finished her sentence.

There was a loud rumbling as the brakes screamed. The truck spun around and stopped with a huge crash. The impact knocked them all into each other, confusion and shouts filling the compartment before the room swayed and the horizontal became the vertical. Several persons hit hard and cried out in pain.

"Inez!" Rafael stood up, braced against the compartment wall, formerly the ceiling, trying not to step on the moaning bodies around his feet.

"*Aqui.*" She reached for Che, assured herself he was fine. Her nurse's training came naturally to the front of her mind as she checked her neighbors. "Is anyone hurt?"

After a moment of silence, one woman began to cry, frightened her husband would not wake up. Others complained of twisted ankles, aching wrists.

Inez and Rafael tried to separate those who were injured from the others. Most tended to those they could reach. Inez used what supplies she could beg from people, bandages torn from clothing, bits of cardboard for bracing. She had no pain medications. People would have to rely on their faith for comfort.

Che uncoiled like a spring, leaping over those on the floor to thump on the compartment wall behind the driver. He bent down and looked through the foot-long opening between the two. "Hey! People are hurt back here. You stupid *pendejos!* What do you think you're doing?"

Inez listened for a response, but there was none. She helped move the man having trouble breathing to the side of the compartment. "Is there a doctor here? A nurse?"

No one volunteered.

An emotional Che was still banging on the wall. "Hey, Coyote! Get back here now!"

"Hush, *muchacho*," Rafael said in his soft voice. "You'll frighten the women." He gestured at Inez.

"Listen!" Che demanded, as the quiet grew.

There was no engine noise, no doors slamming, no voices up front through the thin metal. "Look at this," he said, pointing to the small window near the top of the box, now on its side.

"All right, all right. But calm yourself," Rafael scolded. He made his way awkwardly across the eight feet to where the young man waited, stepping over those who could not move out of his way. Turning off the flashlight, he tucked it in his pocket and bent down to take a look.

Rafael blocked the window with his body for several long moments, shadowing the compartment. The moaning and whispering in the dark brought chills down Inez's back.

Why wasn't the truck running?

What would become of them now?

They hadn't received a lot of heat from the front, but the small trickle had at least pumped in steadily, nearly enough to supplement the body heat from the crowded travelers. If there was no engine, there was no heat. No heat…and they could all die.

The boy sat heavily down. "We're fucked." As Rafael fumbled to get the flashlight back on, it caught a tear running down the boy's cheek. "We're fucked. They're both dead."

A swell of protest rose from those in the truck, the babble nearly overpowering in the enclosed space, on top of the tears and complaints.

Rafael's face was grim. Inez's stomach clutched and twisted.

It was true.

"What are we gonna do now, man?" Che demanded. "The truck's buried in a tree, they're both *muerte*, and this box is locked from the fucking outside. We're fucking dead!"

Several others took turns peering through the small window, too small for any of them to get through, though someone knocked the glass out to give them more air. Most of them sat and prayed, rocking, disturbed, hopeless.

Rafael grabbed the kid by the shirt and pulled him close. "Look, my friend, if we all lose our heads like you, we *will* all be dead. There is a way. We may not see it yet, but there is a way. Knock off the chest-beating. This isn't the barrio. This is life or death."

He moved closer. "If you whip these people up so that they act stupid," he added just loud enough for Che and Inez to hear, "I'll make sure you don't survive. We will need all our wits to get out alive, hear me, boy?"

Rebellion sparked in his eyes, but under Rafael's unflinching gaze, the boy finally nodded. "Yeah. I hear you."

"Good. Now, let's see what we have to work with." The man surveyed the chaos around him, and turned to Inez. "Any ideas?"

She shrugged. "Open the door?"

Rafael looked at her, surprised a moment, then laughed. "Good plan.

Let's get started. *Vamonos, amigos!*" He shone his little light all along the rear door, searching for a weak point, but found none.

"Maybe sheer force." He rammed the door with his shoulder and groaned. "Solid."

"Maybe something to pry with? Anyone have a crowbar? Anything like a crowbar?"

Inez carried no metal in her small duffel, but someone might have. A general rustle followed as people checked their bags. Rafael shone the light to help them as he could, but the light began to flicker and finally faded.

All they found were two small vents, perhaps six inches long and three inches deep, that had been hacked through the fiberglass roof with a saw blade, just enough to allow them air to breathe. Perhaps the drivers had lost other loads previously, their cargo trapped in the box for too many hours, unable to breathe in the heat. Small bits of snow blew in with a wicked chill wind through those open holes, but they were not big enough to climb out.

The light from outside had gone as well, not that there had been a lot from those three narrow windows. But it had been something.

Blizzard winds rattled the truck.

It was black and cold.

They were trapped in a box with no heat, and no help. Nothing else came to Inez but prayer. She slipped her hand in her pocket and clicked her rosary beads through her fingers, reciting the words silently, waiting for dawn.

* * * * *

CHAPTER 18

Crouched in front of the fireplace, Teo carefully stacked two more chunks of wood on the fire. Just feet from the flames, he finally felt warm in two shirts, sweatshirt and a double set of socks.

With his diagnosis, he'd gotten used to frequent chills, but this was worse. The wind lowered the temperature outside and in, and the barometric pressure dropped, creating pain pockets in his bones.

Not much different than a real Chicago blow out the picture window, snow billowed down. The wind swirled and clumped the white stuff, shook it and regrouped it like a sculptor building a texture piece. It was only ten p.m. Tuesday, and already eight inches deep.

If I'd stop looking outside, I'll stay a lot warmer.

Jake Patrin walked up behind him. "Righteous fire you've got there, sir."

Teo smiled. "Boy Scouts, four years."

"Lots of us learned good skills there, it's true." The caretaker chuckled and then cleared his throat. "Local news desk is calling for nearly two feet by noon tomorrow. Freak storm of sorts, least for this time of year. A shame this happened the week you were here. Usually we end a session with a big barbecue out in the hut."

"So we'll be snowed in?"

"Least a day or so." The middle-aged man leaned a hand on the mantel, studying the scope of the snow through the window. "But it's supposed to warm up by the weekend. So if we can hold on three, four days, we'll be all right. Old Uncle Jake will make sure you're all fed and toasty." He smiled and moved off, heavy boots echoing.

Teo gave the snapping fire another couple of adjustments, then stood and closed the glass doors, brushing off his hands. Patrin was right, of course.

If it had been mid-January, with a prospect of weeks of severe weather ahead, there would be reason for alarm. What might have been a truly desperate situation was obviated by the supplies they had brought with them and the news that it was expected to warm up soon. Judy had provisioned the place for the eight of them for a week. They should be just fine.

His gaze was drawn inexorably to the view outside. The crystals continued to spiral dizzily down, large as quarters. He'd lived in Chicago for years, but he'd never seen it come down so thick and fast.

Something's ominous about this.

He dragged himself away as the complaints of those returning for post-dinner conversation preceded them down the hall. A hot cup of green tea in hand, he took the chair closest to the fire, idly sketching on an abandoned pad of paper.

Most of the others congregated in the lounge area, clothing layered as he was. Patrin had left a fresh pot of coffee, but most sipped ruby wine. Teo stayed where he was, nestled a little closer into the knitted rust throw behind him.

A cry of triumph came from the kitchen and the Harmonics trainers burst into the lounge, marshmallows in hand. "S'mores, anyone?" Zanna asked with a giggle. Will handed Judy a long fork and the bag of marshmallows while he opened the graham crackers.

"Oh, my God, are you kidding? I haven't done that for years," Judy said, laughing. "My kids used to insist, every camping trip." She shook her head, lost for a moment in memory. "Anyone else?"

John Kirk joined them—more for the company of the cheerleader than the gooey sweet goodness, Teo guessed—and Annike opted for a sole square of dark chocolate. The others alternately looked outside and protested the weather.

Will looked up from the marshmallow he had wedged between two graham crackers. "Wish I'd brought my cross-countries. Skiing on a fresh fall is awesome."

He grinned at Teo. "Do you ski?"

"When I can. I've been too busy the past couple of years, but I did enjoy it."

Annike's usually strident tone smoothed to silk. "Remember that week we spent in the French Alps, Mitchell? Out on the slopes at first sun, that crisp air..." She paused dramatically until all eyes focused on her again. "We were so much in love."

Mitch laughed and launched into a funny story about their pregnant ski instructor. The others roared and joked, each trying to top the outrageous vacation tale before. Teo tried to relax, coping through the pain as the day's exertions took their toll, setting his bones to aching.

Will perched on the stone corner nearest Teo. "You look tired," he said with a gentle smile.

"Long day." Teo nodded. "And I've got nothing to compare." *At least nothing I want to share with this group.* "Some of those stories are stretched farther than Jane Fonda's cheekbones."

"Tall tales, hmm?" Will leaned back, amused. "I bet you hear some wild stories. Do you defend criminals? Gory things?" His eyes flashed with envious delight.

"No, nothing so dangerous." Teo sipped tea, almost embarrassed to share his work, anything but exciting. "I file patents. For new inventions, particularly in the area of computer art and graphic design."

"Ohh." Obviously disappointed, Will sat forward, his attention wandering to the others.

John Kirk elected to play a spirited game of Texas Hold 'Em with Judy and the other half of the Harmonics team. He'd made much of his snakebite, hobbling round, gaining sympathy, especially from the young blonde.

The caretaker declared him on the mend, however, so there had been no need for a trip to the hospital. An ice pack for swelling and a handful of aspirin later, he was willing to settle in, leg propped up, and have a few dark ales with his co-workers.

Mitch, Annike and Cattrin chatted in thick-padded Adirondack chairs on the other side of the fire, wine glasses in hand. Cattrin seemed to always be playing catch-up as the two senior partners detailed their travels through the glamour capitals of Europe.

They made their success look so effortless. But they'd certainly paid dues, despite being born to privilege. And neither was perfect.

While Mitch was a total leader, brilliant, incisive, and able to get what he wanted from people, he over-focused on himself. He booked his vacation time well ahead and insisted he was entitled to it, passing off all but emergencies to the others.

Annike could be a poster child for "self-involved," but she, too, was sharp as a woodcutter's axe and a consumer of people, particularly underlings. The staff turnover in Chicago was horrendous.

Teo's gaze slid to Cattrin Odeon. She was the master manipulator. Cattrin wanted to be admired, almost desperate in her quest for attention. So she cultivated the secretaries and paralegals, remembering each birthday and event—and expected adoration in return.

None of the three seemed to have a true, warm connection with people, the ability to have a genuine conversation with someone who couldn't be persuaded to do something for them.

If that's the price of stellar success, I'll remain on the B list.

After several hands of the game, Zanna abruptly got up from the table, her usual bright smile fading. "I'll be right back," she promised as she hurried out toward the bunk room. Will watched, somber-faced, shaking his head as she vanished.

"Something wrong?" Teo asked, curious.

"Huh?" He seemed genuinely startled someone had noticed. "I—ah. Zanna. She gets…migraines sometimes." He shrugged uncomfortably.

"That must be awful." Teo knew he should get out of the chair and go to bed, but it seemed like the effort would take more strength than he had.

"Yeah." Will mulled over something and watched the door where the girl had exited.

Teo raised an eyebrow but didn't pursue it further. None of his business.

John Kirk and Judy refreshed their drinks while Zanna was gone, gazed for a few minutes out the window, speaking softly, as the snow continued to fall. When she returned, she settled into her chair, picked up the deck of cards and started to deal.

"Let's get this butt-kicking on the road." She laughed merrily as the other two rejoined her, slowly relaxing into the flow of the game once again.

Will studied the players for a few minutes from across the room, then suddenly drained his cup, rising to his feet. "I think I'm headed to bed. Good night, Teo."

"Sleep well." As the young man left the room, Teo wondered what had disturbed him about his partner. Clearly he and Zanna were not a couple. Teo could read body language well enough to see that. Was it her flirtatious conduct with John Kirk, or was there more to it?

Again, none of my business.

He forced himself to his feet, his face steeled against the jerk of pain, avoiding Cattrin's inquisitive dark eyes which swiveled in his direction. "Good night, all," he said. A lukewarm chorus of "Good nights" followed him down the hall.

In his room, Teo checked his precious medicines, took a handful of vitamins and got two extra blankets from the closet for his bed. He left his socks on. He read from a well-worn copy of Heinlein's *Stranger in a Strange Land* for a few minutes until his eyes got heavy, then he turned over and tried to forget about the accumulating white outside.

* * * * *

CHAPTER 19

Hours passed in the dead truck. The darkness settled into their bones along with the sharp pain of cold, which had thoroughly penetrated the uninsulated truck walls. The Mexicans opened their packed bags and put on their clothing, every bit they'd brought. Most of it was thin, but at least wrapped in layers, they stood a better chance of staying warm. Others broke out matches, candles and little flashlights they'd brought as well, conserving their use to moments when the howling of the wind outside terrified them.

As the temperature dropped, even less was said. Inez shivered despite five shirts topped by a new light blue sweater, a gift from her mother before she left. The man next to her wasn't shivering—or breathing. Rafael urged them to move closer together, to maximize gathered body heat. So many never moved.

For the first time Inez considered the possibility of death.

They'd all had a turn, those who wanted, to look out the broken window through the front where the dead men lay. The panorama outside the truck was not encouraging: a faint light as the white snow reflected an insipid moon. The blizzard swirled about them from time to time, though, blocking the light. Snow threatened first to envelop them, then blew away in huge white clouds.

How much snow could there be? Inez had never experienced such frigid fury.

Suddenly, an older man, thin even in his layers, burst out in a string of curses, and in frustration, started ripping at the floorboards, now the left side of the box. A small circle of terrified people gathered around him, urging him on. Others had laid down near the front; they hadn't gotten up again. Inez hoped they were just sleeping, but she didn't believe that.

As the mayhem grew louder and stronger, Inez and Rafael watched from the corner nearest the door. Hope faded, as Che and the others slammed repeatedly against the locked door in the dark without a breakthrough.

Resentment bubbled up in her. This wasn't what she'd expected—not part of her bargain. *I intend to live in America… and I will live. I will.*

"How long do you think it will be till someone searches for us?" Rafael asked quietly. The two of them huddled together, having made an unspoken pact to be reasonable as long as possible. "Surely the *coyote* expected to pick us up. He will be looking for us, won't he?"

"How can one see anything in this snow?" Inez sighed softly.

Just another knot in the growing string of disasters this trip had become—a gamble she perhaps should not have taken.

A triumphant yell issued from the middle of the circle. Rafael shone his second small light over that way. The man, hands bloodied, held up a long piece of metal he had pried from the floor, shaking it at the ceiling. "Take that, God!"

"Good work, *amigo!*" Che called out. He squinted in the dim light. "Where will that work?"

People scrambled over those on the floor to the front window and to the two small vents on the sides of the truck. One was on the ground and would be no help. The other waited just overhead. "Here! Try here! No, here!"

Che lifted the man up onto his shoulders to reach the six-inch vent in the former side of the truck. "Can you pry it somehow?"

The man tried several times but the lining of the vent only bent the metal shard. He cursed and dropped it, grabbing a shirttail to wrap around his hands to stop the bleeding. Inez didn't know how he could go on.

Che stiffened, his jaw tight. "No! We will not die here like trapped rats." He grabbed the metal and stabbed it into the wall behind him, the fiberglass former ceiling of the truck. To Inez's surprise, it went through. After a shocked hush, the group cheered as Che used the metal piece to carve an opening into the ceiling.

"Of course," Rafael said. "There is no need for the ceiling to be thick—it bears no weight in the transport."

When Che was through, the others went mad with joy, clapping him on the back and yelling. His success spurred the others to action. Several of the men had heavy metal belt buckles that became battering tools, and they continued to punch and kick and stab in shifts as minutes, likely hours passed, until the hole they made gave them a view of the world outside.

"*Madre de Dios,*" Rafael said as he looked out. Inez peeked, too. Snow lay deep around the truck and more coming down. The wind blew in, sharp as a knife on her exposed skin.

Rafael turned to them, their faces a pale reflection of the white outside. "If we leave here, my friends, where will we go? We do not even know where we are."

"We're not fucking staying here!" Che waved his arm at the floor of the truck. "Do you want to end like these? At least out there, we may have a chance."

The others agreed with Che.

Inez did, too. Here they would die for certain, a slow, numb freeze claiming their very bones. Out there, something could happen.

"Rafael, we must go. Together. There may be a house, a restaurant, something along this road," she said.

Che pushed forward to look out again, stepping on the edge of the torn place in the ceiling to gain as great an advantage as he could. "Lights!" he cried. "Over there—lights!"

He shivered violently. Inez had seen what he'd brought with him, a small pack. She wondered if he'd had to leave in a hurry, running from the father of the girl he'd impregnated. He'd need warm clothing to go out into the maelstrom. Her gaze was drawn to the others on the floor, many better dressed. They no longer needed what they wore. It would do them no good.

Che, at least, had the desire to live.

The dozen who were still upright took turns, glimpsing their small ray of hope, the lights across the field. As the sun came up, Inez imagined she could see buildings there, too.

Rafael finally nodded. "With the help of God we will reach that place."

Che snorted. "We'll do it ourselves. God hasn't exactly blessed us with this trip, you know? I'd rather depend on myself." He looked around. "And my friends here."

His warm smile included those in the truck and they cheered faintly. Inez wondered if they realized what they would face in the snow outside. Most had never encountered this kind of storm in their lives. The cold alone sucked the heart dry.

They continued to punch out inches of the fiberglass until the hole was large enough for all of them to shimmy through. Che went first, landing up to his knees in the snow in his flimsy sandals. *"Madre!"*

Inez finally did what had to be done, pulling a heavier jacket off one of the dead men.

"Here!" she called out the opening, and she tossed it to Che. He eyed the coat suspiciously, but slipped it on and turned the collar up around his ears, zipping it up quickly before he jammed his hands deep in the pockets. He flashed her a quick smile of gratitude.

"Wait!" she called, and she threw the dead man's heavy shoes as well. Che stepped into those and turned his back against the wind.

Rafael had watched Inez thoughtfully, and finally he did the same with several of the others who'd had heavier clothing, and packs with some food. After he helped lower the survivors from the truck, he handed out the borrowed treasures to those on the ground. Inez waited until last. She tried one last time to revive some of the others, but Rafael shook his head.

"We will be lucky to survive as it is, *hermana*. We should not hold ourselves back carrying these with us if they are already too weak." He surveyed the bodies, indecision on his face despite his words. "If we find help, we can send someone back for them."

Inez smiled, knowing the faint hope of his words was all there could be. "Then I am ready." She gathered a few of her belongings, tucked them into her pockets.

Rafael lowered her carefully into Che's arms, who smirked as he had her under his control, if only for a few seconds. "With all those clothes on, I see what you will look like when you are old and fat," he teased.

"Idiot." She elbowed him, and his cold hands let her slip to her knees in the white softness, jostling her. *Madre!* It had been bad in the truck but it was much, much worse here. The wind, full of thick flakes, sucked each breath away.

Rafael landed heavily behind her. "Link arms, friends!" he shouted. "Stay close. Head that way."

His voice was stolen by the wind, but they all took a bearing on the lights. Determined, they bent their heads, fortunate, at least, that the wind came from behind them, and trudged toward the only landmark they could find in the blinding whiteness.

* * * * *

CHAPTER 20

The snow swirled in the early morning, more because of the relentless wind than current precipitation. Jake had been up before dawn, the howling air ripping him from sleep as ice crystals tapped on the windows. He'd made the perimeter round of the house, all except for staff quarters, checked the pipes and the locks, then put on the coffee.

Damn.

Just…damn.

As much as he'd said to reassure the guests the night before, Jake had to admit to himself that he'd never seen the weather blow up quite like this. The winter storms he'd experienced were bad, but usually more gradual, and it never stayed frozen for long.

But when he'd first come out to the Ranch, his NA sponsor John White Horse had come out to see the place. John had told some stories— flash floods, blizzards, drought –trying to help get Jake prepared for what to expect from the weather. They'd met in person several times after that, sometimes here, sometimes down in Santa Fe. But they talked on the phone at least weekly. More than that on the bad days.

Jake poured half a cup of coffee without waiting for the brew cycle to be done and gulped it down, then shrugged on his cold weather gear, headed out to confirm the garage was safe and sound. He'd secured it all the night before, but he wanted to double-check. *Ain't my place. Check it twice, like Santa's list. Just to be sure.*

The wind ripped the door from his grip, flung it open against the wall but didn't break the glass. *Holy Christ.*

He wrestled it closed, then pulled his hat down low and his collar up before his breath was stolen away. There'd be some branches down, a real mess to clean up, before this storm was done. He hoped it was nothing worse than a broken window or two.

Jake couldn't see the path as his boots slid in over their tops. The sole security light on the garage/barn building had paled in the blinding snow, but he fixated on it and made his laborious way. The heavy door slid up, well-oiled, and he closed it again quickly, surveyed the large room. It was ten degrees warmer inside than out, but that wasn't saying much.

The Ranch's red Chevy pick-up was parked to the far right. He hadn't plugged in the battery—no need with such a short duration of bad weather. *Roads like they are, no need to go no place anyway, son.* The tools were hung up neatly on the front wall, and he debated taking some of them inside in case of an emergency.

What emergency? he asked himself. "Maybe someone will use the wrong fork for shrimp."

He forced a chuckle to his own bad joke, and checked the fuse box and the location of the generator, in case the power went out. He lifted the phone receiver, something he'd neglected to do at the house, and frowned as he heard dead air.

And the bad news begins.

But with any luck, that would be the worst of it.

All being well otherwise, he braved the storm again, trudged back to the casa and hung up his wet things before he went for a second cup of coffee. He saw the thin male attorney was there by the fire again, looking pinched and cold.

"Hell of a blow," he said, in an effort to be friendly.

The man returned a gentle smile and set aside his sketches. "I haven't been brave enough to look out yet. Everything intact?"

The caretaker nodded. "Looks to be." He warmed his hands on the cup. "Sleep all right?"

"Long enough, anyway."

Teo gave a little wave as Will popped his head around the corner.

"Hey!" The Harmonics trainer went straight to the window, marveling in the view. "Oh wow. Oh." He turned to them with a wide grin. "Jake, you got cross countries here somewhere? If this lets up, the powder will be awesome!"

"Sure. There's a rack out in the utility shed for guests. You're probably a what, size 10?"

"Nine or ten, yeah. That would be great."

Clearly energized by the thought of getting out in the white stuff, Will piled a huge bowl of granola with fruit and milk and sat at the counter to eat it, watching the swirl outside. He glanced at Teo. "You want to go?"

"No, thanks. I'm not really a fan of cold weather." Teo moved closer to Will, leaning against the counter. Jake wondered if he'd hit on the kid, then chided himself silently for the thought.

Will stopped chewing a minute, puzzled, then finished his bite, pulling on a thick Aran sweater. "But I thought—aren't you from Chicago?"

Teo laughed softly. "Guilty. But look at the firm, I've got Denver,

Chicago or D.C." He shrugged. "If they get an office in Houston or Miami, I'm there." With a smile, he helped himself to a flawless golden banana. "Meantime, the culture in Chicago is hot. So I learned to dress warm."

"I hear you. I hear you, man. It's on my list of places to visit, for sure." Satisfied, the young man dug into his breakfast again.

Jake murmured noncommittally and then got into the cupboard to set out a few other choices for the late risers. After three days, the stores seemed to still be fairly full, though they'd gone through supplies without much thought to conservation. *If they're stuck inside for a while, it will go faster.* With nothing physical to do…

Well, there was always the alcohol.

There it was again.

He sighed and closed the door.

"You should have some breakfast," Teo urged. "We have plenty. I know Mitch said you were welcome."

"That's okay. I've got to go back out and check the shed in a few minutes." Jake smiled. "I usually wait till I'm all done, then kick back and watch Judge Judy." He winked.

Teo raised an eyebrow, then smiled. "Guilty pleasures."

"I like her style. She kicks ass." The caretaker refilled his coffee, hearing footsteps coming down the hall.

John Kirk, Mitch and Zanna arrived simultaneously. They each did the double take out the window, then made a beeline for the coffee pot. Jake greeted them and then set up another pot to brew, half-listening as they struck up a conversation on snow sports with young Will.

Mitch seemed as thrilled as the young athlete that skis were available. Teo went back to his pencil work. The little blonde bounced over to the window and peered out with wide blue eyes before she returned to the counter for a toasted English muffin with fruit preserves.

"I can't believe they want to go play in it," she said to John Kirk. "It's like—do you remember that movie? *The Shining?* Where the people were trapped in by the snow and…." She trailed off at the mocking look on his face.

Jake was annoyed at the big man's attitude. "Don't you worry, little lady," he said. "We'll survive without resorting to axe murders. The cupboard isn't empty, and you've only got to hold out three days."

She flashed him an awkward smile before she took a seat next to her co-worker, who elbowed her gently, teasing.

"Besides," Teo interjected, "Mitch said we couldn't bring any work. We actually have time off."

Jake glanced at the senior partner, who had suddenly taken a determined interest in regaling Will with a story of mythic proportions from an old Vermont ski trip.

But Jake had things to tell them. *Best get the bad news over with.*

"Folks, I have a little announcement. Nothing to worry about, but seems the phone lines are down. It happens out this way, especially with this wet snow. Linemen'll be out soon as the road's passable."

As Mitch protested, Jake held up a hand. "Yes, that means fax, computer, everything. Can't be helped, friend. Glad you all had your outdoor activities wrapped up, aren't you?"

"Nice," John Kirk drawled. "No cells. Great idea, Mitch." His smile took the edge off the comment, but all the same there was a hint of concern there.

Mitch fumed. The vista outside lit up as the sun broke clear over the horizon. The snow beyond the glass sparkled, the wind rippling its surface.

Zanna looked over at Jake, eyes troubled. "What if the power goes out too?" she asked.

"I'm sure they've got a generator," John Kirk said. "Most places in the mountains, resorts, the like, they have backup. You got backup, don't you, man?" He looked at Jake.

Jake nodded, more to reassure the girl. "Gennie's out in the barn if we need it."

"See?" the man smirked. "I'm sure we can find ways to stay warm."

The expression on his face made Jake uncomfortable, though none of it was his business. The little blonde had been trying to get the tall man's attention practically since the moment they'd arrived, and the snakebite had given her the perfect excuse. John Kirk was the kind of man who'd be flattered by that attention. Jake was sure he got plenty of it, with his rugged looks, not quite centered but broad jaw, thoughtful gray eyes... The little blonde would be just his style.

Annike and Cattrin drifted in then, soft layers of sweaters and perfume, feet in fluffy puffs of slippers in pastels. They bemoaned the weather, one dark head, one light, side by side at the sink, staring out.

"Mitchello, what are you thinking, dragging us out here in the elements like...wild dogs?" Cattrin purred with a sweet pout. "If we wanted to be lumberjacks, we would not have spent so much money on law school, yes?"

John Kirk snickered. "America was built on the strength of robust frontier women, Catt. I'm sure you're up to the test. Hell, we get this much snow half a dozen times a year in Denver."

She cocked her head like a sparrow, bright eyes studying John Kirk. "Why do you think I don't work there, hmm?"

Wanting to get back to his work, Jake hesitated in the doorway. Judy had been his real contact in the group, and he'd hoped to see her before he left. Talking to her made sense.

But tensions were mounting. Mitch and Annike shared an animated conversation in hushed tones. It continued for several minutes, and then Annike stood, glaring down at her former husband as the other conversation fell into a lull of silence.

"If you were anything like a real man," she said, her voice icy as the wind outside.

She waited a few seconds to make sure the jab hit its intended mark. Mitch's face froze, stunned. She stalked out back toward her room. The senior partner stared after her, then looked to see who had noticed. The others quickly found other things very interesting, except for the foreign one, who watched avidly.

"Will!" Mitch barked, prodded into action. "Let's give those skis a try." He snatched a cup of coffee and went to get dressed in outdoor gear.

Will grinned, delighted to find a co-conspirator. He turned to the lounge. "Anyone else?"

Cattrin wriggled, charged up by the conflict. "Out there? No one in their right mind would venture out into that!" She shivered and went to find an apricot and a few almonds for breakfast.

That seemed to please the kid even more. "All right. We'll be back. You can all watch and see what you're missing." He vanished in the direction of the back forty.

Jake put his coat back on and took a dry pair of gloves and boots. The comments about the generator had concerned him. *Better make sure the old gal will turn over.* As he lurched out toward the garage, the two men in bright colored jackets and gloves glided across the yard toward the arroyo. They seemed to be enjoying themselves.

Pete had been right, Jake thought. *Crazy gringos.*

* * * * *

CHAPTER 21

Inez stumbled again, she had lost count now of how many times, her small dark flat shoes no match for knee-deep snow. She hadn't been able to feel her feet for a long time. If Rafael hadn't had one of her arms, and Che the other, she would likely have given up, sinking into the blank whiteness.

They'd lost several people already. Four, five or more had slowed and vanished. Che had an older woman clinging to his other arm, shouting encouragement to her. Three women had been there when they'd left the truck.

Rafael had one still, a man from Juarez called Trini. He'd had two. Two more men stumbled on behind them, propping each other up. Several had fallen away, one at a time, but Inez and the others slogged on through the cascading snow. Her guilt for leaving them had been assuaged by her own drive to survive.

Once the faint sun was up, it illuminated the buildings, their terra cotta tiled roofs a deeper red. They approached the house across a wide open space, making faster progress in occasional breaks from the wind.

There had been lights. Someone would be there.

Surely they would be welcomed in, if they didn't die first.

Even Che's inner fire had been nearly smothered by the relentless white flakes falling down on them. It was cold. *So cold.*

Her face stung at first, the snow and wind now feeling hot against her skin. Each breath of frozen air burned her throat. She tried not to think, just move her wooden limbs forward. She was so tired—she just needed to stop, to rest. *Please God, please Mother Mary…just get us to the door. Please. Please.*

She gradually realized the snow had in fact let up, as if in answer to her prayer. The farm buildings seemed in ready reach, some two hundred feet ahead of them. If she'd been at home, it might have been easy to sprint that last distance. As it was, she was unsure if she could make ten more steps.

Rafael urged the man he was pulling along to hurry. "It is only a short way now, my brother. Do not let your spirits down!"

Inez was past shivering, her eyes half closed. If she could just stop for a few minutes....

Her face suddenly stung as Che dropped her arm long enough to slap her awake. "Come on, my beautiful girl...you and me, we have a future ahead. All those beautiful bambinos we will make. Don't die on me!" He grabbed her again, shaking her in a bone-wrenching wave of pain that served its purpose.

"S-s-s-top," she whispered, tears coming to her eyes.

"Come, Inez Suela. We must survive," Rafael warned. "Be strong."

"They probably have guns," Che mumbled. "If they have guns we should be ready to fight. We can take them. We are lions."

"You are a f-fool," Inez whispered, lips cracking.

"There! Look!" Che stopped, pointed, at two brightly-dressed figures coming from the largest building, moving lightly on the snow, sliding on long sticks, what she guessed must be skis. All of them stared in disbelief.

"They think it is fucking vacation. Look!"

The sight of other life stirred them all, and the seven moved forward, past the drifted snow that covered the arroyo. Inez realized in her mental haze they were all covered in white, bits of ice frozen to their clothing like glitter balls. It was possible they hadn't been seen. The two figures, one in yellow, one in blue, moved toward them, she couldn't tell whether they were male or female.

Che shoved Inez behind him, hooking her arm through the woman on his far side, and the two women clung to each other, barely able to maintain balance. "I'm going after them," he said.

Rafael reached for his arm. "¡*Párelo!* Stop! It is not the way—"

Che ignored him. "I'm going," he said. He stamped his feet hard to knock off the accumulating snow and skirted around behind scrub brush weighted down with the wet snow. Trini followed him, the same desperation in his eyes, along with one of the other men.

The wind carried the voices of the two from the *casa*, men's voices, speaking in English. Instinctively afraid of being discovered, she and the other woman huddled together behind Rafael, hardly daring to look. They were some thirty feet away when Che and the others stepped out from behind the scrub. The two skiers stopped, the one in yellow pulling off his knitted hat to take a long look at Che and his friends.

The two groups of men stared at each other, frozen like ice statues.

"A great day to play in the snow, huh?" Che called out.

The Americans glanced at each other, then back at Che. The older one, the one in yellow, replied to Che, but Inez didn't understand him.

The other man, barely a man, she thought from the brilliance of his clear eyes, took in the rest of them, huddled together, terrified. His jaunty red cap and thick blue winter coat stood out against the white as did his cheeks, reddened from the wind and cold.

"W-Who are you?" he asked slowly.

The older man muttered something under his breath.

The young man looked from one of the Mexicans to another. "Illegals?"

Inez shivered. She wanted to plead with the men to take them back to their warm home, but she didn't know how.

"Got room for a few more in your fine vacation palace?" Che asked in Spanish. He smiled broadly. The coat he wore hung from his shoulders— it was quite apparent it wasn't his. Inez took a look at them all, unsavory characters from the start, if appearances were everything. Her mother would have let none of them cross her threshold.

The older man unbuckled his skis and stepped off them, holding both poles tight in one hand, almost like a sword. He gestured back the way they'd come and said something about the road.

Che shook his head, smile fading. "No. No, we can't go back there. They're all dead. We need help. *Ayúdenos.*"

The younger man twitched. He'd understood one word, at least. "*Muerte?*"

"*Sí, muerte,*" Che said. "And we, too, if we don't get inside soon." He held out a hand to the older man, who swiped at it with his poles. Che's jaw set. He glanced at Inez, who shivered so hard she could hardly stand. Why couldn't these men see what they needed?

The young man spoke up. "*Me llamo* William. Guillermo," he said slowly, as if it had been some time since his lips had formed around Spanish words.

"Yeah? Well we freezing, Guillermo," Che spit, in broken English. "Maybe you people could get us some house, some food at your nice hacienda, huh?"

The older man glared at Che. "We don't want criminals in—"

"Criminals?" Rafael protested.

The big man stiffened, making Inez's grip on his arm falter. "What's happening?" she asked him quietly.

Before he could answer, Che stumbled across the distance between him and the older man, falling into him and yanking one pointed pole from his hand. The other disappeared into the snow. Both men fell to the ground.

"Hey!" the younger one shouted. He ran over to help up his

companion, standing half in front of him 'til he'd become firm on his feet once again.

Rage flared in Che's eyes. That dark streak of anger she'd seen in the truck had been tapped again.

"I show you cree-mee-nals, *amigo*!"

He stabbed in the direction of the Americans with the pole. "My friends and I are coming into your house. We choose not to die. So can you."

What would Che do? Kill the man? How would this convince those in the house to let them in?

Inez's thoughts whirled in circles like the snowflakes around them. "Please!" she called out in English to the men. "Please?"

When they turned to look at her, Che grabbed the first man by the collar. His makeshift blade was suddenly in his hand instead of the pole. "Be calm, brother, and show us the way in," he said.

The man struggled, but Che put the blade to his throat.

"Don't make me do this," he said.

The younger man had started forward when he realized what had happened, but the appearance of the blade obviously confused him. He held out a hand to Che.

"Okay, let's stop," he said in English, slowly enough for Inez to understand. "Let him go."

But Che was possessed by his anger. His hand shook, and a thin strip of blood appeared on the man's chin.

"We gonna die if we stay here. If you think I am cree-mi-nal, so what? Meester rich man. Look at this coat. These gloves. Rich *gringo*."

The young man stripped off his gloves and held them out. "Let him go, man. Let him go and you can have these." He caught Che's look at Inez. "Or I'll give them to her. But you can't kill him." He held them in Inez's direction.

Che stamped his foot in the snow, then weaved a bit. "How I know you're not a liar? I think I keep this knife here. Then we see."

The young man hesitated, then frowned. He stood, poised, like he wanted to charge Che and the man he held hostage, but he couldn't bring himself to do it. "Mr. Kadeen, just tell them they can come in. I mean, look at them, they're half frozen. If we send them away they'll die. We can deal with legalities once we're inside."

"They're not supposed to be here anyway," the older man said between clenched teeth. "It's not our problem."

Inez's heart sank at the hostile tone of their words. At least the younger man seemed to have a heart. This one was as icy as the land around them.

Elsa groaned, then went down in the snow. No one had paid much attention to her while the argument progressed, but she'd apparently had more time in the cold than she could stand. Rafael bent down to lift her out of the snow. The event seemed to galvanize Che.

"That's it!" He shook the older man. "Take us inside now, or you'll die along with us."

The young man in the blue coat shrugged. "Don't hurt him," he said. "That won't help anyone, not you or your friends."

He crossed over to help Rafael hold up Elsa, who was now unconscious and a dead weight.

Che brandished the metal. "*Vamos, muchachos.*"

He went forward, clutching the rich man, half for support. Inez followed him, forcing one foot in front of the other by sheer will. The young man called William stripped off his gloves, his hat and his coat and shared them with the Mexicans. When Inez put on the gloves, she couldn't even feel them passing over her skin. She'd never seen someone with a frost injury before, but skin so numb it had no sensation? That was bad.

The group staggered and lurched up to the house, and William opened the door, heavenly warmth reaching out to welcome them. *They'd made it.*

She dropped the outside layers she wore onto the floor. A sea of startled faces greeted them, and a few screams, after Che entered with his hostage, the sharp metal held very close to the man's neck. He barked at Trini to bring him a chair, then he shoved the man into it, glaring at the others as he gripped the man's collar.

"Anyone messes with us, the rich man's dead!" he announced in Spanish.

Shocked expressions showed Inez they gathered the import of his words from the makeshift knife at least, if not the threat itself. Well, if they had guns, this would be the time they'd show them.

She reached into her pocket, hands burning with the cold. She'd put a small book, a New Testament, there when she'd left the truck. It wasn't there now.

Her brain fuzzed out as her legs chose that moment to give way altogether. She tumbled to the floor. Only the fact her limbs were nearly frozen kept the fall from hurting too much. Rafael, his wary gaze on the well-dressed men and women before them, tried to get to her, but he stumbled as well and caught himself on the back of a polished wooden chair.

However Che had arranged it, they were safe now. They would be warm. They might live.

She dimly heard William tell Che to calm down. Someone called for blankets and warm water. Then the darkness came and swallowed her up.

* * * * *

CHAPTER 22

Please at his successful start-up of the generator, Jake flipped off the switch. The screaming from the *casa* filled the sudden silence. His head swiveled back toward the house. *What in sweet Jesus' name....*

It was the women. He could tell from the pitch. Hell, maybe someone'd found a dead mouse in the kitchen closet. Only one of the dangerous things in there. Muttering a curse under his breath, he pulled his pea coat closed to trudge to the house through the knee-deep snow.

He came through the mud room, doffed his coat and boots, slipped on softer- soled shoes as the rumpus continued. The door between the mud room and the kitchen area was closed, but he could hear a babble of voices, some of which he recognized, others....

He frowned.

Someone was yelling and cursing in Spanish, male voices he didn't recognize at all. It didn't sound like a performance, one of his guests playing a role for effect. Jake didn't speak Spanish well—hell, it had been nearly twenty years since his time in Central America—but he knew enough to understand it was a threat.

Christ on a rutting Harley.

A quick look around the mud room showed him more than he'd noticed at first. Twice as many clothes as there should have been. Much more snow melting in piles than two men would have brought back. Something was seriously not right.

He scanned the room, but found nothing he could use as a credible weapon. Jake picked up a rough-handled shovel; it was the best he had. He leaned close against the door, listening a moment more to see if he could get any clue what might be going on, but there was only more yelling. The young kid from the team urged people to be calm, something about the fire. No help. He took a deep breath and swung the door open.

He was unprepared for the scene that faced him. He came in behind several huge dirty men in the kitchen, along with the kid, Will. The big boss, Kadeen, was pinned in a chair with something shiny at his throat, a wild-eyed wetback holding his shoulder. Everyone else cowered on the far side of the pass-through, watching with horrified expressions, eyes he was sure were as wide as his.

The scene seemed to unfold in a jerky slo-mo. As the door opened, the two bulky men closest to him turned and saw him. It clicked in his mind that the men weren't fat, they were bundled in wet clothing. The kitchen floor was covered with water and mud, so he planted his feet firmly.

He raised the shovel, but the guy holding Kadeen yelled and made a movement with the shiny object.

"I'll kill him," he said. The look in his eyes left no doubt he'd do it.

A dead guest was the last thing Jake needed. He had no truck, he had no phone, and he was holding an old shovel against a crowd of intruders who had knives. His best weapon was to keep his wits and try to talk everyone down from the ledge.

He half-lowered the shovel, summoning up as much of his rusty Spanish as he could remember.

"Okay, let's all take a deep breath. No one needs to get hurt."

The hot-eyed young man still didn't seem convinced.

Jake set the shovel down behind him, but within arm's reach. He lifted his empty hands. "Come on, let him go."

Judy's anxious face appeared in the pass-through. "The two women have collapsed. I'm not sure if they're breathing."

The older blonde made some comment to the other fancy woman, *sotto voce*, looking down on the fallen. Judy shot her a look, then turned back to Jake.

A spurt of angry Spanish burst from the man holding Kadeen. Jake eyed the two men closest to him, both of whom looked worse for wear. Will pushed Jake forward.

"This man...uh, *el hombre es, um... medico. Ayuda.* Doctor. Um...."

"Son, I ain't no doc—"

"Shush!" Will hissed, leaning in to the older man. "You're the closest we got. These people aren't thinking right, and I don't want anyone to get hurt."

Jake stared at him. "You think I'm going to psychoanalyze the Tequila Kid there and get him to play nice, you've got another think coming, son."

Will bit his lip. "I know it sounds crazy. The whole situation is crazy." He glanced out the pass-through. "Maybe he'll back off if we give them some help. Hot food, medicine, warm socks, whatever. They've been out in the snow for hours, I think. Please, Mr. Patrin."

Jake took a deep breath. "Fine."

He studied the men, one at a time, seeing the white patches on their skin, the layers of wet clothing, the occasional shiver. *Definitely frostbite.*

"Let's do this. We're gonna help you, all right? Take care of things."

Right up until I can bash someone with that shovel and get control of my casa back.

He looked at the guy with the weapon, which seemed to be a piece of sharp metal. "Okay, *amigo?*"

The guy pulled his soaked hood back. He wasn't even as old as Will. His eyes, though, were tired and empty as an aged man's. "Hokay." He gestured with the metal, leaving Jake a clear impression what would happen if Jake tried anything.

Judy and Will, now they were sensible people, they'd not panic or get distraught, and they wouldn't be likely to try anything stupid. The situation had to stay calm, at least until he could sort out what the hell was happening.

"Will, why don't you and Judy make some food? *Comida?* Soup, toast, nothing heavy." He looked at the bulky men to see if they understood. "*Comida? Si?* Coffee?" One of them half-nodded, an older man who looked a little shell-shocked.

The flurry of activity as food preparation started distracted the Mexicans for the moment, and Jake turned his attention to the boss.

"You okay, Mr. Kadeen?"

Kadeen started to protest, then thought better of it. *Good for him.* "Fine," he mumbled past a swollen lip.

"All right. Everyone's going to relax now."

Kadeen eyed him with contempt.

What the hell does he think I'm going to do, go all Bruce Willis on these guys? I've got a roomful of potential victims right over on the other side of that wall. If I get a chance I'll take it. Otherwise, I'm playing these cards one at a time.

He left the kitchen in Judy's hands and moved into the lounge. The two dark-haired women on the floor had faces blotchy with the white patches that indicated frostbite. He knelt down, felt their clothing, soaking wet still with melting chunks of ice attached. They each had a pulse, slow and thready. A glance at their drenched street shoes and thin pants caked with melting snow let him know the feet would be in the same or likely worse shape than their faces. *Christ.* His medic years had been served mostly in lands around the equator. *But there was that TDY at Thule, Greenland. That Higher Power loves to screw with us, don't it, though?*

Judging by their frozen, distant poses, he guessed none of the lawyers had any inclination to help.

"Anyone like to tell me what's happened here?" he asked casually, hoping the lawyers would take that as an invitation to engage. "Anyone?"

"Aren't you going to call the authorities?" the tall blonde woman said, voice dripping with condescension. "You've got a home invasion in progress, Mitch is bleeding, and they're threatening to kill him. Calling the police would seem to be a priority."

Jake shot her a look, wondering if she could really be that clueless, or if it was cultivated. "I told you the phones are down. We're on our own, sister."

Besides, the way you've been talking to him, I don't understand for a minute why you're worried about anything happening to him. Surprised you didn't take care of him yourself.

He got to his feet, looked around again, and took a deep breath. Will and Judy were setting out cups and plates with food. The Mexican men fixated on the smells and steam coming from the dishes, so he cleared his throat and knocked on the counter to get everyone's attention.

"All right, *muchachos*. You need help."

Through rusty Spanish, helped by Will's occasional word or two, and gestures, he managed to convey that the women would be all right, but that the Mexicans needed dry clothing and medical help.

"How will we get them to a doctor in this blizzard?" Judy asked. She handed out plates, snatching her hands back when empty, her face white with tension.

"We can't." Jake was tight-lipped. "I was just out in the garage. My truck's dead. In the winter I keep the battery plugged into an outlet, but I didn't think it would get so bad this late in the season. We're going to have to treat them ourselves."

The young man with the weapon watched him like a starving hyena. Jake held out his empty hands.

"Look, *caballero*, you need to let that man go. *Let him go.*"

He pointed to the women, to the food.

"We will help you. But you need to let him go." He could read the other's gaze, saw thoughts running through him, and kept eye contact.

"I'm Jake," he said, pointing to himself. "Jake." He looked pointedly at the kid. "Any of you speak English?"

The men stared at him. The two in the back grabbed full plates as Judy offered them, and started shoving food in their mouths. Finally, the big man leaning on a chair seemed to grasp reality enough to answer, studying Jake with some puzzlement, his face now cherry red. His clothes were as worn and wet as the others, but at least he wore work boots. *Maybe he wouldn't lose his toes.*

"Speak English okay," the man acknowledged, with a glance at the one holding Kadeen.

"*Como se llama?*" Jake had his eye on the ones in the kitchen, counting on the people in the other room to react if the status of the women changed.

"Rafael Diego."

Jake nodded, one man to another. "Rafael, do you understand frostbite?"

The man chewed that over a moment, shook his head.

Great. Just great.

"Okay. I need to put all of you in hot water. *Agua caliente.*" He mimed putting in hands and feet. "All right," he said over his shoulder, "now some of you others, can you go charge up the hot tub? I need it between, I don't know, 100-110 degrees. It's on, but not quite that high. Lots of towels. And I want dry clothes for these people. I got some clothes in my room, should fit these men."

The blonde lawyer glared at him.

"As much as y'all hauled in here," he added, "I'm sure you can spare something. We've got to do this in the next few minutes or these folk are gonna start losing fingers and toes."

No sound of movement behind him.

He turned to eye them. Framed by the picture window, the two fancy ladies stood like statues, arms crossed. The guy with the snakebite had a cold simmer going on; Jake guessed he was working up to some kind of grandstand play. Who else was there?

The little blonde wandered out of the back about that point, looking more sleepy-eyed than she had earlier, now wearing gray sweats and a huge oversized navy sweater that hung almost to her knees. "What's going on?"

Jake shook his head at her. *Hung over. He'd bet his week's pay.*

"Look. You and…." His eyes slid around till he caught the pooftah. *Theo. Teo. That was it.* "You. Hot tub. Now. You ladies get some clothing. *Please.*"

He turned back to Rafael as the two well-dressed ladies didn't move a muscle. "We need to carry—" He mimed picking up the women. "—Them to the *agua.*" He added a questioning look. "Okay?"

Rafael nodded. The man's hands were white-skinned as well. "You too. *Agua.* But first, he needs to let the man go." Jake eyed the kid. "Now. I need to check him, too."

Rafael shot off something in Spanish to the kid, whose mouth fell open before he went on a verbal rampage. All the Mexican men jumped in on it, the angry staccato exchange mostly a mystery to Jake. Clearly the kid ended up in the minority and after several minutes, he stepped back, jammed the weapon in his pocket, and raised his hands.

"Hokay, *gringo*," he said with a sneer.

Jake stepped forward quickly and reached for Kadeen, intending to pull him to safety. Instead Kadeen yanked back from Jake's touch with a look of disdain. He straightened and walked around the counter, stepping over the two women on the floor, to join his partners. He angrily sloughed off his jacket and boots, then gingerly felt his face. The ladies twittered over him while Jake did a slow burn.

You're welcome, he thought. *Jerk.*

Judy slid a plastic bag full of ice across the counter to Kadeen. The blonde attorney reached for it, and handed it to the boss, who took it with a grudging nod.

"You don't have any way to contact law enforcement?" she demanded.

Jake frowned. "We'll have to wait till the lines are restored. Meantime, I need help taking these people down to the sun room." He pinned the ex-football player with his gaze. "Can I count on you?"

"Me?" John Kirk gave him an odd look. "After what they did to Mitch?"

"A group of dangerous criminals!" the little Asian one squeaked.

"Lord, I ain't got time for this."

Disgusted, Jake looked over his shoulder at Will and Judy. "There's a first aid kit out on the mud porch to fix up your boss."

Jake turned to the Mexicans. "*Vamonos.*" He scooped up the one girl himself—she hardly weighed anything—and headed out, barely aware if anyone followed other than Rafael, who brought the second woman.

Judy came after him, wiping her hands on one of the dark blue kitchen towels. She frowned, her ordinary face drawn with concern. "Where did the Mexicans come from? I thought the border patrol was cracking down on people crossing over. How could they possibly get here? And in this weather?"

"Beats me."

He and Rafael set the women down on cushions near the hot tub as Teo went in search of more towels and clothing. "I'm guessing they're illegals. That right?" He pinpointed the big man. "*Coyote* bring you across the border?"

Starting to show signs of pain and weariness, Rafael looked uncomfortable,. "*Si, senor,*" he finally admitted. "The trock, she wreck in the snow. *Coyote,* he *muerte.* We try to find shelter." He shrugged.

Jake nodded. *Poor bastards.* "Hot enough?" He looked over at the little cheerleader who was testing the water. The hot tub bubbling filled the room with a low rushing sound.

"Yeah. It should be fine."

"All right. Here's the game plan," he said, looking at each of them in turn, hoping he recalled the protocol. "You got to do it fast. Drop 'em in the hot tub, ought to do it, bring the tissue up to room temp pretty quick."

"I thought you weren't supposed to fast-warm those kind of injuries," Judy said. "Can't that lead to shock or even a heart attack?"

He gave Judy a sidewise look. "This is Army best protocol, ma'am. Only thing we don't have here they had at Thule was some IV morphine. This is gonna hurt like hell."

Rafael grunted in protest, but Jake was already moving. He stuck a hand in the water, checked the in-pool thermometer. He remembered with a frown the guys who'd been the patients at Thule, their reactions to the sudden warmth. He hoped like hell the Mexicans wouldn't hurt anyone.

At least we don't have the young hothead with us…of course that means I have no idea what he's up to. Why didn't he come down?

Zanna cleared her throat, a guilty expression on her face. "Hey, Mr. Patrin, can I talk to you for a minute? Please?" She gestured to the other end of the hall.

"Now?" Annoyed, he glared at her. She seemed intent, in a way that piqued his curiosity. "All right. Just a sec."

He turned to the lawyer waiting with Rafael. She seemed like a good soldier. *We'll find out.* "We need their clothes off. Everything but undergarments. Understand, Judy?"

Judy appeared a bit overwhelmed but agreed, gingerly touching the sodden garments of the woman closest to her. "Sure. Is this your wife?" she asked Rafael. "Or…this?"

"No. *Mi esposa…* in Juarez."

He gave her an understanding smile as he helped her remove the clothing, the layers smelly and drenched. He pointed to the two and named them. "Inez. Elsa."

Jake walked the ten feet down the hall to where the cheerleader waited. "I'm kind of busy right now, honey—"

She squeezed his arm. "Look, I don't have morphine but I've got…some other things. I heard you say you wanted something for bad pain." Her blue eyes met his, very serious. "But you can't say you got them from me. I mean it."

Jakes wished he could be surprised, but he'd called this one from the get-go. *Takes one to know one.* "All right. Let's see what you've got."

"Here." She reached in the pocket of her oversized sweater and handed him an unlabeled prescription bottle with a dozen tablets. "It's Oxy80s."

Unprepared for that, he dropped it like it had been a snake. *Sweet Jesus! Right here? My old drug of choice? And she just hands them to me like it's a roll of friggen Life Savers?*

"Don't you want them?" Her face clouded over. She bent down to retrieve them, holding them out to him again.

"You have no idea, darlin'," he said, in a split second knowing exactly how they'd taste on his tongue, exactly how long it would take to get the rush, especially if he'd scrape the covering off that made them extended release. He hungered for it, especially under all this pressure. Hell, he could almost sense the way the world would slip away if he had two or three. He shook his head, tried to clear it. "Come on."

"But don't you—"

"You carry them!" he barked, turning on his heel and walking back to the hot tub, arriving just as the women started to wake up. They shivered as the air of the room, while not cold, hit their wet skin as they were undressed. Jake grabbed a glass from the wet bar behind him and ran cold water in it. On empty stomachs, it should hit them quick.

"Give them each two," he said, his hands trembling. *Right there, they were right there and all he had to do was—*

"Give it to them!"

"All right." The young woman seemed puzzled, even hurt, by his reaction, but did as she was told, the women choking the water down, becoming a little more aware of their surroundings.

Rafael watched with a frown. "You drog them? For why?"

Jake looked up at him, wishing they had more time. *And a damn interpreter.* "Because this is going to hurt."

He studied the bare limbs of the women, the signs of the onset of tissue damage to their legs real and evident, and nodded to the others.

"See all those white and gray areas? They're frozen. We're going to drop them in here and melt them real damn quick. They're not going to like it. But it's the best way to save them."

The one Rafael had called Inez started to panic. "Rafael!" she screamed, struggling out of Judy's reach. "What's happening?"

The big man reassured her (or so Jake guessed from the soothing tone. Teo returned, looking away from the mostly naked women as he set down the clothing he'd appropriated in a dry spot.

"All right," Jake said, nodding to Rafael. "Now!"

They lowered the women into the hot tub, the surface of the water steaming a bit as the bodies displaced the water. Jake knelt close, supervising as Judy and Zanna made sure the women's damaged parts were soaking, despite their laments and whimpers. Even if he had the medical training, he thought it best to let the women handle the women out of respect.

"How long?" Judy asked. Lines were drawn in her face, reflecting the agony of those writhing in the water. "Oh my God. This is awful, can't we do something else?"

"This is the right way, Army best," Jake insisted.

Those were the good old days, when someone else was responsible for everything and we just took orders. Now hey all think I know what to do. And I haven't got a plan.

Things were out of control in his *casa*. Somehow he had to get them back. He could only guess what was going on in the kitchen and lounge, but there was no question he'd snagged the easier half of the group.

The lawyers weren't happy with him, and he knew that would reflect on his job. And the little girl behind him had a handful of heaven that would make it all disappear…

He closed his eyes a minute, ignoring the nausea, and got hold of himself. "Girlie, give the big man there a couple of those pills, because he's next."

"I do not need drogs," Rafael insisted. "I am a man."

"Yeah, we'll see," Jake said. He watched every second as the man refused the pills on Zanna's outstretched hand, and swallowed hard, his own fingers twitching. Hunkered down by the edge of the tub, Jake looked away from the naked bodies, glancing at the overhanging plants, seeing some brown leaves that would need trimming despite the humidity.

Small things. Small things he could fix.

These women, he could fix.

The rest?

Where's that Higher Power when you really need it?

Back to small things.

"There—don't let her climb out!"

He looked over to Teo, as the big man—Ralph maybe—knelt down next to the tub, soothing the distraught woman. "What did you find?"

Teo held up several flannel shirts, several pair of heavy socks and some women's knit pants. "Miss Michaels had some things. I hope they're big enough. The shirts can be worn over in layers, though."

"It'll have to do. Too bad the fancy ladies can't be tapped for some of their thick sweaters," Jake grumbled.

When the time had passed, the dripping women climbed out, shivering violently. He instructed Judy and Zanna to pat-dry them thoroughly without rubbing, using the thick soft cotton towels. When they'd finished, they applied aloe vera cream from the first aid kit in the nearby bath. Then the women shakily pulled on their warm dry clothing. When he inspected them, he found them pale and weak, but clearly on the way back.

Standing up, Jake looked at Rafael, several thoughts crossing his mind at once. "Two things, pal. You're next, so strip down. We'll move the ladies out to get something to eat. Teo can supervise if you need anything."

He glanced in Teo's direction, and the other man nodded.

"And second—where the hell are your *compadres*?"

* * * * *

CHAPTER 23

Davi Pilar's truck, straining through the deep piles of snow, moved like his ancient dog Umberto toward the meeting point. He was hours late. Accursed weather. The only hope that kept him going was that they were hours late as well, caught in this freak storm.

Cold as it was, his heater worked fine. The smell of his sweat filled the cab of the truck, his nerves frayed by the rotten weather and the thought of losing his precious ten thousand dollars. The radio had gone to all static half an hour before. The white flakes stabbed at his windshield, reflected brilliant in the headlights, looking like something out of one of those space shows on bad American television.

Why hadn't the fat man fucking called him on the cell? Give him the location of his fucking human cargo? Huh? Had he run off with them all, made some other arrangement, after they'd made this deal? He couldn't imagine too many other men would be willing to drive endlessly around in this blizzard to meet up with that fat man.

Just one. Just one desperate man.

The road signs were barely visible in the blowing snow. He strained to see them. He'd made all the right turns. He'd followed the route he'd marked in red magic marker. That was the highway, and he'd crossed the intersector, so any minute he should be at the place.

His tires thumped over something dark in the road and he swerved into his skid, trying to maintain control as the truck threatened to vanish into the white. Only an iron grip on the wheel prevented him from flying off into the ditch. He skidded back into his lane, only to find two more dark humps in his path, jarring his tires as he couldn't avoid them in time and slid sideways.

Davi slammed on the brakes. It wasn't until he climbed down from the cab he realized the depth of the snow on the pavement, up to the tops of his old yellow work boots. The wind was wicked, and he shivered as the first cold current of air blew up under his thick stained Carhartt jacket, through his thinning hair.

He'd left the headlights on to help him navigate, and stalked over to what he'd hit. He'd have to move the fallen tree or branch out of the way before he went on. He kicked at it. To his surprise, the lump was soft, gave under the pressure of his foot. He leaned down and poked at it, realized belatedly it was a person face down in the snow. Jerking back, he tried to digest that information, reached down and grabbed the thinly covered wrist. No pulse. The shock sent him upright again, breathing hard as he tried to comprehend what any human being would be doing in such a place.

"What the—" What else had he hit? He climbed into the cab, grabbed his flashlight then stomped down the road behind the truck. Checking the dark huddle, some twenty feet beyond the back of the vehicle, he saw it was another Hispanic man, wearing multiple layers of clothing. Also dead.

Dead men in the snow? Were these his *pollos*?

"*Madre de Dios!*" Pilar searched the immediate area but didn't see any more. He got a sick feeling in the pit of his stomach. Where had they come from, these dead men? Was it coincidence? He didn't think so.

He staggered forward through the drifts, walked along the road in the direction from which he determined they must have come, his high-beams lighting the half-filled footprints in the snow. The blizzard finally started to slow. After he'd walked several minutes, he saw it. A box truck on its side, a ragged hole torn in its flank and two more dark figures in the snow near it.

"*¡Ah, chingado!*" The wind tore the words from his mouth and they went tumbling away over the silent drifts. He hurried forward, ready to choke the fat man, but when he shone his light through the front windshield, shadows deep in the faint light, he could see it would make no difference. Bastard.

He leaned against the cracked glass for a few minutes until its chill burned his face. Ten thousand American dollars, gone. Just gone.

His flashlight flickered as he stood there contemplating what to do. It was all a waste. Unless....

He hoisted himself briefly to have a look inside the truck. There were bodies inside,. as well, and the smell of too many people too close. But the trace of footprints lay all around the back of the box, where the snow was protected from the wind. Someone had milled around, more than one, and their tracks headed away. How many? How many had lived?

Davi Pilar growled. They were his. He'd earned them. And he meant to have them.

His foot kicked something in the snow, something not a body. He shone his light on the reflecting snow, found something roughly four inches square, picked it up with freezing fingers. It was a book of some sort. Frowning, he shoved it in his pocket.

He stomped back off through the deep snow toward the dark hulk of his truck, meaning to follow them. Pulling himself into the driver's seat, he kicked the snow off his boots, flipped on the inside light to take a closer look at the book.

It was a partial Bible, in Spanish. One of the truck occupants must have dropped it, he thought. He opened it to a place where a daisy had been dried flat between the pages, the imprint still remaining, though the flower itself much have fallen out. Crazy *pollos*. They probably need every bit of the protection of this silly book, he thought mockingly. He flipped to the inside front cover and dropped it as if it had been on fire.

I didn't see that.

He awkwardly bent down and picked up the book, his fingers trembling. Inside the front cover were the words he had seen. *To Inez Suela on her confirmation. Love, Nana Ramirez.*

Inez was on that truck.

Like a shot of lightning, his brain went off, as he remembered the fat man's brother mocking him about a surprise. Was this it? What a surprise it was!

Remembering the bodies in the truck, he decided he had to know. He grabbed his handheld light and clambered down out of the truck. Was it her? Was she dead?

He stopped and rolled over the bodies on the ground, one at a time, checking. Not her. Not her. Not…her. Hardly feeling the cold in his effort, he climbed up on the truck and steeled himself against the smell before he lowered his lanky frame inside. There were so many dead…so many…

But not Inez.

As that penetrated his brain, he looked once again at the footprints in the snow. Then she'd gone where the wind had taken her.

Determined to find her now, he clumped back toward his vehicle. As he approached the dark hulk, the lights faded and went out. *How could this happen? I've driven it for hours!* Disgusted, he knew from his five years in the States that cold did crazy things to vehicles.

He cursed the worthless truck and the fate that had brought him here and given him the chance to lose her all over again. He kicked the tires until his foot ached. As sunlight came over the horizon, he hauled himself up onto the bumper of the truck, taking a long look around. There. He could see in the distance a large ranch or group of buildings, and a number of dark lumps in the snow between here and there, very much like the ones he'd hit in the road. They hadn't all made it. But maybe some of them did.

That's where they were. That's where he'd get them back.
And his money.
And Inez.
Just a matter of time.

* * * * *

CHAPTER 24

The lights were too bright.

Back in the kitchen, the voices swirled around Inez like the murmur of women in church, indistinct but laced with feeling. Her head spun, and she was grateful for the caretaker's strong arm who held her up. He was no doctor, but he was a good man.

The soup tasted so good, full of chunks of chicken and vegetables with rice, warm and filling. Her feet ached dully, but whatever medicine she'd been given made it seem far away. He left her propped on a stool in the corner, then he walked away to speak to the others from the *casa*.

After a staccato discussion, the man Che had hurt, his voice loud and angry, sent the caretaker back to the whirlpool. The others spoke among themselves, the big-shouldered man behind them watched Che, Trini and Rai, taking no notice of her at all.

She ate and listened, her limited English gleaned from pirated television programs and magazines. The tone taught her much more about the state of things: dark and troubling.

Che caught her eye once, and winked with a teasing smile. He'd eaten soup in noisy gulps, as if it might be taken from him at any moment. He still rumbled about their status as second-class citizens in America.

Idiot.

Why could he not simply be grateful for their survival?

As if in response to her thought, Che came over to take her hand. He raised it to his lips to kiss it as if they'd been at some fancy dance. "*Que linda,*" he said, his blood-stained hand squeezing hers, his skin flushed and dry.

"Are you never serious?" she asked, annoyed, pulling her hand back. "You could have killed that man."

"I'm very serious, *nena*. I could be dead at any moment. I want a good memory on the top of my soul."

The other Mexicans behind him snickered.

How could they laugh about the situation? It was frightening, and sad, not funny at all. "I know you are not that much of a fool."

He stiffened, and she returned her attention back to the last few bites of soup. The spiky-haired Anglo entered with Rafael from the hall that led to the tub.

"Your turn in the tub for the frostbite," Will reminded Che and the other two men.

"I'd rather talk to the pretty *chica*," Che's grin dismissed the young man.

Inez cleared her throat. "It would be better to make sure you are healthy. If you don't tend to your hands, your feet, you can lose fingers and toes. Do you want that?"

Inez half listened as they glanced at their white fingers. Painful as it had been, the treatment the caretaker had given them was likely the best thing. Inez had never dealt with frostbite in her training, but it had been in her books.

After a hushed conversation, Che turned back to the young man. "They say they like it here."

The woman with glasses offered them all more soup, but none of them accepted. Che caught a peek at the food closet, its louvered door half ajar, and walked over to pull it all the way open.

"*¿Puede usted creer esto?* My family didn't see this much food in three paychecks." He looked up and down at the pretty bright packages, the tins of specialty items, and finally spied what interested him most.

"*¡Cerveza, mis amigos!*" He reached in and pulled out a couple of six packs of Killian's Red, studying it curiously. The Guinness seemed to floor him altogether. "*¿Los americanos beben el aceite del motor?*" The other men laughed and reached for the less alien beverage.

Inez frowned. It was a recipe for trouble, that's what it was. The last thing they needed was alcohol. Before she could protest, another crisis showed its ugly face.

"Che!" Trini grabbed his elbow and pulled him out of the closet. One of the Anglo men stood in the doorway to the kitchen, a fireplace poker in his hand.

After a moment of icy recognition, Che scowled, stepped in front of Inez. "Get behind me, *muchachos*," he said. "Ain't no heroes today." The other two Mexicans shuffled behind him in their clunky wet boots, dark eyes glaring with hatred.

The woman with glasses froze, leaning up against the sink. Only her hand moved as she shoved a big knife into the sink out of reach with a loud thunk. The sound caught Che's attention, and he grabbed the woman's arm, yanking her in front of him as a shield.

The spiky-haired one stepped quickly in, hand raised against the poker in case the big Anglo decided to use it. "Let's not be hasty, okay?"

He looked nervously over his shoulder at Che. "No one wants to hurt anyone. At least I think that's true." He looked at Che. "Right? *Si?*"

The young bantam eyed the gathered group, simmering. "I don't stand with a metal stick. That's the *Gavacho*'s fear talking."

"Whose side are you on, Starlin?" the man growled. His hostile gaze took in those in the kitchen and he lowered the poker but didn't put it down, didn't step back.

"I hope I'm on the side of reason," Will said.

His voice carried a conviction that belied the fingers' tremble Inez could see from behind. She was grateful he would speak up for them, even if she did not understand all he said.

"None of us asked for this situation. But we're in it. We can look at it like an extreme exercise." He forced a nervous laugh. "Time for all that teamwork to pay off, right? We can come up with options—"

"This is bullshit." The man Che had attacked tossed the ice pack onto the counter with a sharp crack. He glowered in the pass-through, his lip's swelling finally going down. "Those men assaulted me and now they're holding Judy hostage." His steely gaze zeroing in on Che. "We're not going to tolerate these tactics, Paco. Let her go. Now!"

Two well-dressed women came up close behind the man speaking, he who was obviously *jefe* here. The pretty blonde stared, frightened to have lost control, it seemed to Inez. The other, the dark one, had eyes that hardened to obsidian.

Rafael and Trini exchanged several staccato bursts of Spanish, chiding Che for his passion. After an intense sixty seconds, Che released the woman, stepped back. "Hokay, gringo. Reech man. Hokay." He grinned at Mitch, grabbed a beer and drained it like he hadn't a care in the world.

Mitch beckoned to Judy and the one called Starlin. "Come out of there, now. Both of you."

Will started for the door, but Che seized Judy's arm before she could get out. "I think she will stay with us." He focused his dark gaze on Mitch, clearly taking this as a challenge.

Frustrated, Inez interrupted. "It's not smart to make enemies of these people, Che. We don't know how long we will be here, what we might need from each other." She stared at him, wanting to get through before blood started flowing. "If you want me to beg, I will. Please, Che. Maybe they can help us."

Che looked at his buddies, broke up laughing, almost on the edge of hysteria. "Help? We are past help, pretty *chica*. We are pretty well fucked. Meester reech man calls the *policia*, we get thrown in fucking jail and then sent back to Mexico. Right? What can you do about that, hah?"

"Sounds about right to me," the man with the poker grumbled.

The little dark one, she who looked as foreign as they, slinked up to the window and stared hard at the Mexicans. "You don't belong here," she said.

Trying to head off more violence, Inez caught Che's attention. "We can wait for the snow to clear and then find our ride to freedom. The coyote said Davi would be there--"

The young man, now starting to look worn and irritable, dismissed her. "*Promesas. Promesas sin setido.*" Disgusted, he let go of the woman, and she escaped to the other side of the window, not waiting for a further invitation.

Cattrin smirked. "*Usted es tan estúpido como usted es sucio.*" She took a cup of coffee and stalked away down the hall.

Hesitating by the counter, Starlin blinked in surprise. "Wait. She speaks Spanish? Wait!" He moved toward the boss man. "She should come back. She can translate."

The boss growled. "No. No, Starlin. We're not playing this goddamned game. Come out of there. We're not helping these people to do anything. They'll kill us as soon as look at us."

He waited half a minute, saw he wasn't going to move, and his jaw snapped tight. "Cattrin's right. They're terrorists. The only way to win is not to play."

He gave the Mexicans a final glare, then walked after the one called Cattrin, with a jerk of his head to his friends, who disappeared after *El Jefe* into the hall.

As the tension eased, Inez's legs went weak and she pulled herself back up onto the stool where the caretaker had left her. Che opened a second bottle by smacking the lid off on the edge of the counter, then took a long drink, watching Inez defiantly.

"You go find the others," he said to Will. He waved a hand in the direction Patrin had gone, with a mocking smile.

The young man hesitated, wrestling with some decision, then stalked off down the back hall.

Che watched Inez as he sucked the liquid from the bottle without stopping. When the beer bottle was empty, he burped loudly and tossed it in the wastebasket.

Inez had to do something. If Che would not go down to the tub, perhaps he'd listen to her here. She crossed to the sink and ran it full of hot water, then added a little liquid soap. "At least warm your hands."

A distrustful flicker passed through his eyes, but at last he swaggered over to stand next to Inez at the sink, never looking away as he pulled up his sleeves and put his hands in the water.

His face paled, with a hissed "*Hija de la puta!*" The muscles in his jaw tightened, worked as he dealt with what Inez knew to be bad pain. But he fought to keep his hands still, not jerking them out of the water, never looking away.

Inez didn't look away either, a faint smile coming to her face. "You are a brave one," she whispered to reassure him. Her eyes watered in sympathy. "This *will* help. You're doing what's right."

She watched his lips move in silent prayer or a curse, she didn't know which. She was with Che, in some dark place of pain strung out between their eyes. There were no words, but they didn't need any. He knew she supported him. She knew he trusted her. Everything else she shut out for several minutes until the ambient noise in the room gradually brought her back.

The clock showed ten minutes had passed. "All right. You can take them out."

She patted his hands dry very carefully, remembering from what the caretaker had told them not to rub it. The other men watched and drank beer.

"Your feet need the same," she said softly.

He shook his head. "Not now." He jerked his head at the sink, stepped aside as she ran more hot water in for the other men. "*Hágalo.* Trini Raimundo." He was attentive to make sure they soaked their hands fully, especially the older man. Then he stepped out into the other room to retrieve the poker the other man had tossed aside.

Movement outside the window pulled at Inez's attention, and she realized the snow and wind had started up again. "We came just in time," she said, trying not to think about what would happen next. The *jefe*, he would surely be planning something. An attack of some kind. And now Che had a weapon. Where were Rafael and the others?

As if in answer to her question, dragging footsteps sounded in the back hallway. Rafael Diego came in, followed by the caretaker and spiky-haired Starlin. Elsa was not with them; nor were the man who'd brought the clothing and the little young one.

"*Donde esta Elsa?*" Inez asked Rafael.

The caretaker was the one who answered. "She ain't exactly well, that one. Teo's got her in one of the guest rooms keeping an eye on her for now."

Jake walked to the coffeepot and poured a cup. He seemed tense, aware of everything that was going on, but he glanced at the poker, then peered out the pass-through to the other room. "Where's everyone else?"

"Mitch said they weren't playing and they left," Starlin replied.

Jake looked at him with incredulity. "He what? What the hell kind of leadership is—"

Che beckoned to Inez as Trini took a position in front of the open pantry cupboard. Pulling the stool Inez had been sitting on earlier to the far side of the room, away from the sink and the drawers, he gestured to it. "Sit there, Inez."

"Che, what are you doing? I should make food for Rafael, Elsa—"

"Sit on the stool!" he shouted. He slammed the poker onto the seat of the stool. "Sit, now!"

Inez jerked to attention, moved slowly, like in a dream, to the stool and climbed on it, the sudden switch in his demeanor throwing her. Trini and Rai clearly stood in the stance of guards. "What are you doing, Che?"

He gave a weary sigh. "Making sure my people are taken care of. The *jefe* will return soon. We will have his attention, once we are all together and working as one."

Jake moved between Che and Inez, and shoved Starlin toward the back door. "Just calm down, now, son. The storm's gonna pass, and everyone can be on their way—"

The younger man slammed the poker on the counter, fighting to keep his formerly-frozen fingers tight around it. "Here is a news flash, *mis amigos*. The "game" is officially off. This is real. We're staying here, in this room. We will control the food and drink, to make sure the reech men do not starve us. If anyone becomes Bruce Willis—well, they will be the first one to die!"

Rafael shook his head, stepped forward, his tone turning gruffer, deeper. "This is not the way, my hot-headed—"

"Shut up! This is my show now." Che raised the poker over his head, threatening the older man.

"I know you don't want to hurt anyone," Starlin interjected, no sense of challenge in his tone.

"No." Che turned to Inez, and the edges of his face softened, a deep-seated uncertainty practically radiating from him like a fever. Inez could sense it from a foot away. "I don't want to. But we will defend our lives. We deserve to live. Now, out."

"Che, they have been very kind," Rafael persisted, one eye on the poker. He gestured to Jake. "He is the caretaker here. He is very wise. He saved Inez. He could save all of us, if you think before you act, you fool!"

The younger man stiffened and smacked the poker on the counter just behind the other man, shattering bowls stacked there. The sudden noise rattled Inez's nerves and she shrieked. "They have guns, I know it. They will kill us if they can. I won't let them. I won't let them!" he repeated more softly but with conviction.

He eyed Jake Patrin. "You live here, yes?"

Jake nodded. "That's my job." He set his cup down. "I'm responsible for what happens here. If there's something you need, I can—"

Che's face held a calculating look for just a moment. "Food. We need more food."

"There's plenty," Jake said, turned his back on Che for a moment as he opened the refrigerator.

"You know too much," Che muttered. With a swift arc of the poker, he hit Jake across the top of his shoulders, knocking him to the floor. Starlin jumped forward, yelling, and Che swung the poker at him, its tip opening a cut on his cheek. The caretaker, groaning, pushed himself up to his knees, half-facing Che, hand raised to protect himself.

"Che, don't!" Inez screamed.

"He knows where the guns are. I have no choice." Che kicked at the man, knocking him off-balance, then hit him twice more with the poker. He fell and didn't get back up.

Starlin vanished out the back.

"Get him out of here, somewhere where he won't be trouble!" Che barked at Trini and Raimundo. The two men shuffled over and dragged Jake out the way he'd come in, from the back hallway.

Inez watched in horror. How could Che hurt these people after they'd done nothing but try to help? She wanted to object, but her voice had vanished somewhere deep inside her body, wondering if the nightmare had just begun.

* * * * *

CHAPTER 25

Teo sat in a terra-cotta cushioned chair in the spare room, watching the woman sleep. He'd never experienced anything like this, bush-level medical treatment, the women's feet and hands gray with cold, then grading to cherry red as they were warmed in the hot tub. Jake had been detached, professional, even in the face of the crisis. Teo had to admire that.

But what are we going to do now?

The weather had gone bad again. Wind howled past the windows in a sea of white. They were all trapped in here together for the foreseeable future. Were there more Mexicans in the snow who had not yet found their way to the ranch house? How many more?

Now it was about even, between the legal team and the illegals. That what he'd surmised, anyway, that they were illegal aliens. It made sense, especially with all the fluff in the news about predations of the border.

A whole house full of frightened people.

Not a good situation.

He could understand the desperation of those who had broken in, trapped in the white death outside after suffering who knew what other tortures before they'd arrived? Mitch had looked scuffed up but not seriously injured; it could have been worse if that young man with the fiery eyes had cut him.

But what now?

The adrenaline rush of the invasion had started to wear off, here in the quiet, in the back of the *casita*, the noise of the others distant and soft like cotton. All there was here was this sleeping woman, her breath coming slow and uneven. Jake had left her feet uncovered, the skin blistered and raw. Without the drugs to keep her comfortable, Teo was sure she would be in agony.

The drugs....

Teo found it odd the caretaker would have a stash of narcotics at hand. He seemed more controlled than that. In what he'd seen of Patrin, a force propelled him forward, almost against his will. It was not the lackadaisical "laissez-faire" attitude of the drug-addicted.

He'd let the girl dole out the pills, after all.

Regardless, it had certainly eased the task at hand. The women had survived the worst of the treatment. The man Rafael had endured, grim-faced, refusing the drugs. Teo had helped him dress in warm dry clothing, socks and a pair of Patrin's work boots, a size or two larger than the man's feet, which would help keep from rubbing the blisters, if any developed.

Will and Zanna had helped Teo tuck this woman in, Will suddenly concerned with his absence from the kitchen. That had apparently turned volatile, something to do with hostages and Mitch and the others talking about war. Jake had dropped some angry words about the "uppity folk," with an apologetic look for Teo, and the four of them had returned to scope out the lay of the land. Zanna, shaken by the events, had fled back to her room alone, everyone having their own tasks in priority over scolding her.

So he waited here. If anything important happened, he'd find out, he was sure. It was likely time for his AZT. He couldn't wait forever. But for now....

The door suddenly shoved open and Teo's heart skipped a couple of beats. If it was someone armed, he was a dead man.

But it was Annike. Her usually perfect hair was rumpled, face uncreamed and the trace of faint wrinkles evident. She looked at him, glanced over at the woman with disdain. "Come. Mitch has gathered the faithful to arrange a plan."

Teo didn't move. "A plan? What, he's going to storm the castle?"

"Teo, don't argue. Please. We can't just stand by and let this happen. If Patrin won't do his duty to protect his guests, then we need to take action. There is enough stupidity going on here today." The blonde turned and walked out, waiting for him outside, peering down the hallway anxiously.

Curious, Teo rose slowly to appease his aching joints and tucked the blanket closer around the frostbite victim. Then he left her, following Annike back to the room assigned to Mitch. Dark bruises bloomed on the side of Mitch Kadeen's face, and he still held ice on his elbow. Mitch nodded with a crooked smile as he came in.

"Good. Thanks, Annie. Teo, you all right?"

"Better than you, apparently," he replied softly. "No permanent damage?"

"I'm tougher than they give me credit for." Artotech's senior partner straightened his shoulders with a wince, and surveyed his staff. John Kirk leaned against the far wall, tension obvious in his clenched fists, while

Annike sat on a small student-sized desk, Cattrin in the chair next to her. "Back to business. You don't have your cell, do you, Teo?"

He shook his head. "You said no, I left it home." He caught a glimpse of a travel clock behind Mitch, saw it was past time for his AZT by half an hour. His throat closed for a moment. He tried to remain calm.

"Pity." With a frustrated sigh, Mitch paced in the space next to the bed. "We have to be able to raise law enforcement, but the phones are still out."

"They must have some other form of communication," Cattrin said. "Perhaps a radio or walkie-talkies, something."

Mitch nodded. "We'll hunt that out. Where's Patrin?"

"He took the others back to the kitchen to get something to eat," Teo replied, folding his soft hands in his lap. "Dare I ask what happened?"

John Kirk gave him a disjointed version of the scene they'd just been through, his primary focus on the turncoat betrayal of Will Starlin. "I could have had the circumstances under control if he'd listened to Mitch. What the hell was he thinking?"

"Clearly he does not have our best interests at heart. If something happens to us because of his interference, he and Harmonics can be held strictly liable," Annike said quietly.

Teo looked at her in disbelief. "If what you say is true, he may not live either. And you're worried about suing him?"

"Knock it off." Mitch's voice was thick with annoyance. "He's probably doing what he thinks will appease everyone. It's what that kind of person usually does."

The temperature of Annike's voice dropped to subzero. "It figures you would defend him. If you'd done something in the kitchen, you could have taken control of the situation then. If you were half a man--"

Mitch glared at Annike until she looked away, then sat on the edge of the low rough pine dresser. He surveyed them, an effort to maintain control evident in the working of his jaw. "I'm not going to apologize for anything. We're doing the best we can." He eyed Annike. "You have a better idea, let's hear it."

Teo watched Annike wrestle with several suggestions and swallow them unspoken. She shook her head, withdrew into a silent burn.

"Anyone else?" No one spoke immediately, and Mitch turned back to Teo. "So Patrin's up there, with them?"

"He said he'd—"

Teo's explanation broke off at the sound of more yelling in Spanish from the kitchen. Mitch and John Kirk both twitched and stood straight upright. Irregular footsteps came slapping down the hall toward the room.

John Kirk moved to the right of the wooden door frame, ready to pounce on whoever came in. Teo stood as well, wanting to face whatever was coming on his feet.

The sharp edge of tension was released a few moments later as Judy and Will pushed their way inside Mitch's room, breathing hard. They looked around, eyes wide. Judy trembled so badly, Will made her sit on the bed.

"What's going on?" Mitch demanded. "Where's Patrin?"

"Those men, they're crazy. They've got the place locked down tight, and he's got that poker, breaking things—" Judy gasped.

"The young kid took Jake out with that damned poker, had the others take him away somewhere," Will added. "He said Jake knew too much about something. I'm not sure what."

His face was pale, and Teo could see he was frightened too, despite his earlier optimism.

"Probably the local law enforcement, the radio, the phone." Mitch was grim. "They're right, of course. Any idea where they took him?"

Will shook his head. "But they don't seem worried about leaving us loose. I'm thinking we can seek him out while they're busy. The kid seems to be the real hothead. Rafael—the older, heavier set one—he really wants this to be a peaceful transaction." He shook his head. "That's them arguing down there. I half expect the kid to shut him up, too."

Judy glanced at Mitch, and shoved her hands in denim pockets. "The kid's running on empty, I think, and it's not serving him well. He wouldn't come down for treatment, so the frostbite will start to affect him soon. And who knows the last time they slept? They're wrecks."

"They broke out the beer," Will added.

"Oh, stellar." Cattrin's tone was dark. "Before evening, it will be date night in the barrio."

"That could work in our favor," Teo interjected softly. "If they really are stretched to the max, the alcohol could knock them out."

"Or set them into a frenzy. With all of us sitting damn ducks." John Kirk growled and looked as if he was ready to punch the wall.

Will looked around in sudden realization, frowned. "Where's Zanna?"

John Kirk stopped, curious. "I thought she was with the injured people."

Teo shook his head. "She left when they tucked in the woman in the back. I'd thought she'd headed up with you."

"Not with us." Will appeared concerned. "I'd better go check on her. Do you want me to try to find Mr. Patrin, too?"

"Do that. But don't confront any of them. Just come back here. We'll be trying to formulate a plan." Mitch arched his back, stretched shoulders that must be tight with tension.

Teo knew his were the same. *And he needed his medication.*

"Yes, sir." Will started for the door.

"You have a weapon, anything?" John Kirk asked.

Will sighed. "Nope. But I'll keep my eyes open. There must be something around here. If we find Mr. Patrin, I bet he'll know."

"I'll go with him," Teo said, getting to his feet. "None of us should go around alone."

Judy nodded and Mitch agreed. "Absolutely. Come back as soon as you're done." He turned to the others and opened up the floor to ideas.

Teo followed Will for the first hallway, then asked to divert to his own room. He had to take his AZT. Everything now was too uncertain. He might not be able to get to it again for some time. Will accommodated him, waited outside while he gulped some lukewarm water from a glass on his bedside table, and then they went in search of their missing friends.

* * * * *

CHAPTER 26

Inez could almost hear the cold nothingness of the snow falling as she stared out the kitchen window. Being inside was better, but somehow the flow of events was no more in her control than it had been in that noisy cold truck coming from Juarez.

When Che slammed the poker onto the counter, the noise somehow disconnected from the action in a way that frightened her. Her reactions seemed not her own. Her shock and disgust at Che's actions got lost on the way to her lips and she could only stare, read the faces of the others.

After Trini and Rai took the man out, Che and Rafael went at each other in earnest, Rafael picking up where he'd left off in the truck, criticizing Che's lack of forethought.

"And what I am supposed to do, hmm, while you run off with the *gringos,* playing their lap dog?" Che shot back. "One of their men, he came after me with this stick!" He waved the poker dangerously. "Who would have protected the women while you were back there getting all prettied up?"

Rafael's face darkened. "I have had about enough of you, pup." He reached over and grabbed the poker, yanked it hard, nearly knocking Che off his feet. "No one has hurt us here. They have offered us food, water, medical treatment. You have returned only harm."

His look included Inez, trying to enlist her support. "What message does it give to continue this fight, hmm? That we are criminals who intend evil?"

Che clung to the poker like a mad dog. "That we mean business. That we mean not to be shot or thrown back out there!" He jerked his head toward the sliding glass doors.

Inez let her gaze slide to the doors, took a moment to absorb the view, thoughts moving along in her slowed mind like a secondhand ticking. The snow was blowing hard again. The frozen terror was a faded white memory, the details unclear. *It didn't matter now. She was here.*

Grateful to be inside, she wrestled with the fog inside her mind.

She had much respect for Rafael Diego. He suffered at the separation from his wife and children back in Cancun. Even though many of the men who worked at the *maquiladoras* spent their nights out late, partying like they were unmarried, Rafael did not. He had stayed with some neighbors of hers, and they had spoken from time to time. He wrote letters home, laborious letters that took hours to complete because he was not a well-educated man.

"Perhaps you could have reached the same result if you had simply knocked at the door. Even Americans would not have left a dog out in weather such as this," Rafael replied, not releasing the poker.

"Ha! Americans cannot be trusted. Five minutes and here comes *la migra*." Che looked up as Raimundo and Trini returned.

Rafael shook his head. "We should show these people we are not savages."

Che cursed Rafael's mother. "We are not savages, damn it. We are survivors. We came to this place through impossible odds. We have a right to be here. These people, they have everything. Would they give it to us willingly? Hell, no!"

He growled and yanked the poker from Rafael. "So we make sure."

Inez cleared her throat, the coffee sharpening her wits at last. "And what then?"

Che glared at her. "Not you, too?"

"Don't speak as if I betray you, Che." She studied him, his red eyes, the weariness written on his face. "Actions have consequences. You put us all at risk by such acts. When the snow is gone, what will happen?"

"We will—" Che stopped, annoyed. "We'll head out of here. We'll make our own way to Santa Louis."

"We will be fortunate if we are not arrested and sent home in shame. But perhaps they can be persuaded not to turn us in. Maybe they can help us."

"We need—we need to protect ourselves. So we will keep this space. The *gringos* can beg us for their food."

Rafael studied Inez, warmed her coffee from the pot as he got himself a cup. "That boy will be the death of us all. I cannot stop him without putting us all in danger. Not yet."

"He thinks he is being a man." Inez sighed. Her hands hurt again. The drugs must be wearing off. Inez considered a situation where she needed the favor of people who did not speak her language, who held the power of her future in their hands. But the only one taking any action was a sleep-deprived chili pepper of a boy with a big metal stick. Unbelievable.

Che cut off his conversation with Rai and Trini suddenly, head cocked toward the residential area. He growled to his *compadres*, and they scavenged through the kitchen drawers. Rafael again tried to stop Che and he turned, eyes red with weariness and hatred, poker raised.

"Do not push me, old man. If it's us or them—it will be us."

About to remonstrate with him again, Inez stiffened as a voice came from down the hall. "We're coming out!" yelled one of the Anglos.

Her heart sank. Why did they have to bring it to a head so soon?

Damn them. Damn them all.

She looked around the room desperately trying to find something— she didn't even know what—that could bring truce. Che looked back at Inez, something lost in his eyes, then took a stance in the doorway to the lounge, poker in his hand. The other two were in the lounge, in front of him, blocking entrance to the kitchen.

Rafael looked at Inez with apprehension in his eyes. "Go!" he whispered. "¡*Vaya!*" and he gestured to the open door behind him, a clear chance for her to escape. But she couldn't leave.

As much as she didn't want to see it, she couldn't bring herself to go. She had to stay, and watch. What happened next could change their fate forever.

* * * * *

CHAPTER 27

When the light hit Jake's eyes, he groaned. An arrow of agony stabbed down his back, the same area he'd painfully worked during hours of physical therapy after the accident. He was on the floor in one of the back rooms, the third staff bunk, he guessed from the color of the carpet, and it was bright and cold. Real cold. There was snow on the floor. Inside.

The thought made him frown. It was all he could do at the moment. As he tried to relieve the muscle cramp across his back, he found his arms tied behind him and legs bound with a cord from one of the beige mini-blinds. The blinds lay on the floor near him, ripped to shreds, which explained the brightness as the white flakes streamed in the open window.

Open window?

Jake twisted a bit, with a resulting streak of misery, but he managed to look up. The window hung loose from the frame. Through growing fuzziness he realized it was the window he'd been working on the day the lawyers had arrived. The blizzard must have blown it out. Damn it. Not a thing he could do about it from here.

The throbbing continued to push into his field of focus. Jake squirmed around as best he could, trying to take the pressure off his back. He had bigger issues. His houseful of guests was in trouble, and instead of being able to help them, he was here, trapped and tied.

That kid...he hit me. He hit me. God. It hurt so bad, tears welled up in his eyes. *Stop crying. Men don't cry...*

He grunted and tried to shift to a position without stabbing hurt.

What more could he have done? He'd taken the others down to the hot tub, managed to save the one woman in the dark clothing. The man, too, who'd bit down on the pain. The second woman he wasn't too sure about. She'd been very weak when they'd put her to bed. He left Teo to watch over her in case she took a turn for the worse. They'd been exposed for some time, and the snow had clearly been a killer. The woman had shoes suited for going for a walk in the park on a spring afternoon, not tramping through a freak storm. If the little cheerleader hadn't had the—

Drugs.

His brain flashed from one thought to another, trying to dodge the pain in his back, the pain where the goddamned kid had *hit* him—

Drugs. She had a whole jarful.

He sighed. *Have to get out of here.*

Jake pulled on the cords, testing them. They were tight. Not so tight as to cut off circulation, so some thought had been put to his comfort. Maybe there was hope for these interlopers. *Maybe. Or maybe they'd just be half-drunk and lazy.*

Damning his own self for being out of shape, he wiggled around until he could use the wall that faced the window to help himself scoot upright at least, the muscles wrenching as he sat up, another wave of pain. He forced himself to focus across the room onto a photograph of sunset over the California Pacific Coast, maybe Big Sur, dark blue water, black rocks iced with the orange rays of light. He took deep breaths, staring at the fading sun and the faint waves on the water until he controlled the pain again, as the rehab taught him. He could make it without the drugs—

But she had them so close now.

Jake rotated his shoulder once, viciously, purposely. An icicle of hot pain shot through him. It almost shook his thoughts from that sweet relief. They were not for him, never again. Even if he was in the worst agony he'd experienced in the last five years. He'd barely escaped that ride with his life.

As tears came to his eyes again, the sunset blurred but he gradually brought it sharp again, with controlled breaths, counted slowly over the seconds.

All right. Back on track.

He scanned the room for something that could help him get this cord off. He'd left a putty knife on the window sill but that likely wasn't sharp enough. Not much else. He'd probably have been agile enough to get out of this back in his Army years, but it had been a long time since he'd had the fresh techniques in his mind. In his fresh mind.

Triggered by the memory, suddenly he flashed back to the Central American jungles, the oppressive heat and omnipresent buzzing of biting insects, dealing with the Panamanians or Nicaraguans or whoever was considered friendly to America that week. It was the eyes, the eyes of that young kid in the kitchen, echoed in a hundred faces of men desperate and not old enough to consider the long-term consequences of their actions. They just knew they needed something different. They wanted it badly enough they'd kill for it. It was the same look.

But would he kill? Here?

Jake prayed it wouldn't happen. Many factors remained in play. How long would the weather be bad? How long would the food hold out? How stupid were any of the others and what kind of stunt would either side pull in the name of heroism? What did the intruders really want? If it was only survival—why did it have to end badly?

He listened, the sounds of the *casita* part of him by now. The heater cycle kicked in, the water pump running. The lights flickered, but held. Life continued. The pain started to return and he tried not to surrender to the whimper hiding just behind his lips. He'd finally nearly healed and now he'd have to start all over again. *The bastard . The bastard.* He closed his eyes and tried again to get loose, knowing he was just making the stricture worse.

Jake froze at footsteps in the hall outside the door. *Had they decided to finish the job?* He sat up straight, not sure he was prepared to face whatever was ahead. Not that he had much choice at the moment.

A soft man voice spoke, in English. "Where could they have left him? You don't think they would have tossed him outside?"

"Gods, no. That would be murder."

That one Jake recognized. The Starlin kid. "Hey!" he called softly. "In here."

"In here." Several doors opened and closed amid some anxious scrambling, and then Will and Teo stepped into the room.

"Oh my God. It's freezing," Will said. "Are you all right?"

"Been better." Jake's voice was tight.

"The window's open." Teo's face formed a frown. "Maybe they preferred manslaughter to murder." He squatted down next to Jake, looked at the ties. "My friend, you've got that pulled tight. Will, do you have a pocket knife?"

The young man turned back from the open window, which he was trying to seal down, not realizing the entire frame was loose. "Uh, I think so." He dug in his pocket. "I'm serious, Mr. Patrin. Did they hurt you?"

Jake forced a smile. "Everyone all right out there?"

"Far as I know. The Mexicans tossed us out, so I don't know what they're up to." He handed Teo the knife. Teo carefully cut the cords on Jake's wrists and ankles. "The other lawyers are all back in Mr. Kadeen's room, plotting."

"Yeah, I suspected as much." Jake groaned as his arms were released. "Two groups of hotheads…"

The pain raced across the deltoid muscles and a pained moan escaped. "Sweet Jesus help me," he whispered, the muscles on fire.

"Here, come on up." Teo bent to slip an arm around his back, careful not to push on sensitive areas, and actually lifted him upright. Jake was surprised. He hadn't expected the man's slight frame to carry such strength.

"Thanks." He'd never been touched by a gay man, at least one he knew was that way. An awkward moment passed. When Teo released him, he reached for the windowsill, letting that hold his weight.

"No, leave that," he scolded Will, who still hadn't managed to stanch the flow of the snow in through the unrepaired frame. "Just…" He glanced around the room, having a little better vantage point at this moment, and pointed at a plastic bag. "There. Put that over it for now. We've got more important things to do."

Will did as he was asked, then studied the caretaker with a concerned eye. "I can't believe he went after you. I mean, you were helping his friends, those women."

Jake shrugged. "The kid's scared. They all are. They have a lot to lose."

He wished for a hot rice pack, but he didn't have time. He was going to have to play hurt; he'd learned how in his high school baseball days. He could do it.

"He's probably worried I'm going to call the highway patrol."

At Teo's questioning look, he nodded.

"Which I am. If the radio's working. Frankly, I'm not sure anyone can get out here with the roads in this condition. Who knows where these folks were when their truck crashed? If the roads are as bad as the yard, no one's going to be driving. The Mexicans walked here from the truck, I'm guessing a couple of miles, by how long they'd have had to be out in the snow to get that frostbitten—maybe six hours."

"Six hours?" Will looked outside in horror. "In that? No wonder."

"It's understandable, yeah, but it don't make it right."

Jake stretched a little, trying to ease the pain any way he could. It wasn't fading. If he was going to be able to function, he'd have to take something. The image of the girl's hand, holding the Oxys out to him crossed his mind and he had to force it away again. Aspirin, ibuprofen—hell, acetaminophen, if that was all he could find. Squinting, he tried to figure out where the nearest stocked medicine chest was, since the kitchen was between him and his own room.

"Son, will you go down the hall out here to the left about—" Jake counted in his head. "About six doors, and there should be a bathroom with a first aid kit or chest, and get me a bottle of OTC painkillers? Tylenol, aspirin, something?"

"Sure. I'll be right back." The trainer vanished out the door.

"I take it this isn't one of the usual events of a rental week," Teo said, dark eyes deeply sympathetic. "Where are the Homeland Security people when you need them?"

Jake forced another faint smile. He went to the door, checked the view down both corridors. "You best get back to your friends. Look, tell them to let me handle this. I'll call the staties, see how long it might take 'em. They should stay out of the kitchen area. There's heat and water and everything else they need down in the guest rooms. For now."

"You need a doctor." The man was calmly firm.

Jake nodded. "No doubt I do. Ain't a priority at the moment. Making everyone safe? That's something that needs doing. Please. Reassure them I'll get some help as soon as I can."

When Will reappeared, hands full, he broke a real smile. "Good boy."

Will handed him the white plastic bottles. "They're yelling in the kitchen again. We'd better get out of here in case they come looking for you."

"Probably right." Now that he had a moment to consider the situation, he was a little surprised they hadn't left a guard with him. But then these guys weren't firing on all cylinders. They were damaged, sleep-deprived, and totally out of their element. They might have let him get out once. Once he was discovered, he was pretty sure they wouldn't let him have another chance.

What did he have to work with?

The only vehicle that remained was his truck, and it was down. Phones were out. He'd noticed several power fluctuations in the overhead light and the constant hum of the heater that concerned him as well. If they had no power, they'd have no heat. As cold as it was outside, it wouldn't take long for them to be cold in here, too.

"Well, you two should get on back. I didn't get the feel they'd hurt anyone serious, especially if those women we got through the hot water bath have a say. That Ralph, he seems to have a rational head about him. I'll close this door so they don't know I'm out, then lie low. The radio's in the main office; I can take the long way around."

He eyed them. "I'm counting on you to keep the others under control if you can. That will be the key to the whole game."

Will frowned. "I've still got to find Zanna. She split off from the group and I haven't seen her since."

Jake pursed his lips, having a pretty good idea where the blonde girl was, and what she was doing. He cracked open the bottle of ibuprofen, took six and swallowed them dry with a shudder as the edges stuck to his throat. *You'll feel better soon, my man.*

"Best for all of you to stay together until we get their entire agenda on the table, don't you think? I'm thinking this was not an intended stop on their journey and that they'll be on to wherever they were headed as soon as the weather clears. If everyone keeps their head till then, we'll be able to write this off as one of those crazy weeks urban legends are made from."

"Or people will be people, and it will devolve into a potential bloodbath."

Will and Jake both turned to stare at Teo's cold words.

"Dude, that's grim," the trainer said.

"I've learned not to expect good from people. I'm not nearly disappointed as often." Teo gave them a sad smile and turned, slipping through the half-open door.

"Whoa." Will looked shaken.

"Gotta look on the bright side, kid. White hats'll come riding to the rescue, all will be good. You'll see." Jake patted him on the shoulder, a stab across his own shoulder blade as he lifted his arm. "Go find your girl and make sure she's—" He trailed off with a meaningful look at the young man.

Will sighed. "She's probably feeling no pain. It's how she copes lately. She fractured her ankle six months ago, had a bunch of pills and therapy. And then she had a bad break-up with Sam—her ex-boyfriend. And… I— I haven't reported her yet, because she said she's going to get straight here next break we have. She promised me."

Jake nodded, sympathy welling up in him. "You make sure she does, son. Otherwise she'll head nowhere at all. You hear me?"

"Yes, sir, I do." The trainer looked a little younger as relief took some of the stress off his face. "I surely will."

Jake wondered how long he'd carried that particular burden without sharing it. "Go on now." He sent Will along the back to the bunkrooms and then glared at the open window.

I'll be back for you, troublemaker.

He grabbed the pocket knife Teo had left on the windowsill, tucked it into his pocket and limped off for the office, hoping the Mexicans hadn't thought of it first.

* * * * *

CHAPTER 28

The discussion in Mitch's room grew hot and heavy, with six well-educated and culturally loaded minds sharing ideas in a way that put the efforts of the Harmonics trainers to shame. The team had never been so sharp—or so unified.

Cattrin suggested escape out the back across however many acres it took to find civilization, but that thought was quickly discarded as a peek out the window showed they wouldn't be any better off than the illegals had been.

John Kirk and Annike were for fighting fire with fire, storming the kitchen with whatever force they could find. The problem was, they hadn't found much.

Teo returned to the powwow just as Annike stated the whole matter was ludicrous, that the intruders had no rights and should be taken out like wild dogs. John Kirk echoed the tall blonde's determination.

"Taken out with what?" Mitch demanded. His right hand propped up his forehead as though it would burst in pain. With his left, he scrounged through a shaving bag, popped the top off a bottle of ibuprofen. "We've got nothing."

"No one brought a weapon in their suitcase?" Annike persisted, handing him a bottle of water without being asked, as if it were long habit.

"You can't get a gun on a plane any more, Annie," Mitch said. "Hell, after 9/11, you're lucky to get aboard wearing your clothes *and* shoes and carrying a briefcase."

"There's got to be a gun here some place," John Kirk grumbled. "Hell, aren't there groundhogs or prairie rats or something to be managed? A rifle, a shotgun—something?"

"And no phones? And no fax? And no Blackberry?" Cattrin pouted. "Who ordered that, hmm?"

Teo noticed with grim satisfaction that despite the challenge in her tone, her body language belied her bravado: her gaze was downcast and her arms crossed protectively. *She was a coward at heart. Knew it.* Somehow that made him feel better.

Mitch glared and didn't respond, turning instead to Teo. "Where's that caretaker?"

"The Mexicans had him tied up, but we found him. He went down to raise the CB, if he could get to the office."

"Well at least that's something," Annike said drily. "Too bad he didn't do that when this all started."

Judy interjected. "He said the lines were down then. Maybe it wouldn't have been useful."

"And maybe this would be over now if he'd done his job, instead of letting Mexicans take over the place."

Teo looked around the room, not seeing compassion on even one face. "This is ridiculous. Don't you think it would be advisable to settle things peacefully instead of a kneejerk dive for the big red button?"

"You saw what happened out there," John Kirk growled. "You know what happened to Mitch. My God, those people assaulted him with no provocation!"

Judy nodded. "We would have gladly shared if they'd asked—"

"Would you?" Teo challenged her. "Or would you have tried to hold them off with crumbs because of who they are? Second class citizens all, as your attitudes make clear."

They just stared at him. Teo was trembling, indignant, unlike his usual manner. He was always the one who was soft-spoken, reasonable.

What was happening to him?

He'd promised Jake Patrin he'd try to keep a lid on this simmering disaster.

But the escalating tempers around him, the unpredictable and inevitable violence creeping from his companions' pores struck him to his core. It was all so unnecessary in a life he had discovered was much too short. Every minute was precious.

"Teodoro," Cattrin purred. "Be practical. They shot first, in the most figurative sense. We are in the Wild West, you know. We are entitled to the OK Corral confrontation." She smiled winningly as John Kirk grunted approval behind her.

"And if it was you coming to a new land for opportunities, not bought by the slavery of thousands of your ancestors, but in one hot, tight last-ditch run down a lost road where you could make or break your future with one toss of fate? Do you really think you'd drop in for tea in your best tuxedo?"

He glared at Cattrin with all the animosity he'd held against her since the Park Royal. "Are you even in touch with anyone who lives lower than the stratosphere?"

Mitch got up and crossed the room, face slowly reddening.

"That's enough! Get hold of yourself, Teo. No time for hysterics. They've proved they're ready to hurt whoever they feel they need to. So we've got to take action."

Will slipped in the door then, taking a place next to Teo. Mitch raised a questioning eyebrow, but Will just shook his head. Mitch cleared his throat. "Since no one brought back anything of any real use for defense *or* attack, all we've got is what's here." Mitch kicked at the bed. "These posts on the bed frames seem sturdy enough."

"Your wish is my command." John Kirk, clearly wound up with repressed need for engagement, stepped forward, had the bed on one side almost before Judy could get off it, kicking at the bed frame to loosen the post. He wrenched it free, hefted it in both hands as the women watched him wide-eyed.

"You're frelling crazy," Will said. "Those people have risked their lives to escape a life of poverty and degradation. All they want is hot food and water and a place out of a blizzard with warm clothing." He stared at them in amazement. "You can't see that?"

"I'm looking out for the good guys," the tall ex-footballer smirked. "You should, too."

Feeling weak, Teo leaned against the wall by the door, gave the boy a smile for his positive attitude. "I've got nothing against good guys, John Kirk. I'm just not sure I can positively identify them beyond a reasonable doubt."

Annike looked at Teo with pity in her eyes. They might be friends, tolerant of each other's eccentricities. But here they clearly weren't on the same side.

"We're not criminal defense attorneys, Teo. After Mitch, and Jake Patrin, and whoever else, we've got at least a preponderance." She bit her lip a second, then shrugged. "The feather that tips the scales."

John Kirk's face flushed with excitement. "So we'll go out, kick some ass, and then get our happy home back. We can lock the Spics up in the garage till the police get here and then go back to whatever balloon-popping activities the cheerleaders have for us."

Teo eyed him as Will bristled. "I think the term you're looking for is 'wetbacks.' 'Spic' went out with *West Side Story*."

Cattrin's eyes widened, amusement dancing in them.

Stupid woman, he thought. *You don't care who's getting slammed as long as they're lower on the food chain than you at the moment.*

The senior partner pushed past Teo, apparently finished with the debate. "You women stay here. No sense giving them more potential hostages." He pointed to Will. "If you're willing to stand up and do what's got to be done, you come too." Letting John Kirk pass him with his makeshift bludgeon, Mitch headed back down the hall to the kitchen, Will on his heels.

Teo looked at the women, standing in nearly identical poses of affected concern, before he went after the men, despite his lack of invitation. Someone with some common sense needed to go along. He was pleased to hear Judy's firm step follow him.

"I'm not missing a minute of this," she whispered firmly. "There's always a chance to make a difference. It doesn't *have* to end in blood."

Teo smiled faintly. "I was beginning to wonder if I was the only one on hallucinogens there."

The others didn't follow. *Maybe they could spend the time telling cute boy stories and doing each others' nails. Just because the Scandinavian and the Filipino were both two generations removed from the immigrant boat didn't preclude understanding on their part. It couldn't.*

Teo hung back as the lawyers returned to the lounge, not because he was afraid, but because he hoped the confrontation John Kirk Nicholas sought could be avoided.

As they approached the kitchen, they heard muttered Spanish, dark and low. Something crashed and the young man started yelling something. The lawyers pushed forward, agitated, John Kirk in front.

As they rounded the corner, John Kirk sounded a warning. "We're coming out!"

Everyone scrambled for position. Teo and Judy moved into the middle of the lounge, standing on the braided rug. The Mexican woman and the big man waited on the other side of the pass-through. At the entrance to the kitchen, the place they had bantered the last few days away while preparing meals, three Mexicans with bloodshot eyes and strained faces held shiny metal objects poised for attack.

"Oh, God," Judy whispered. "Please, no. "

Teo turned, saw how pale her face was. "You all right?" he asked softly. She nodded, her attention on the knife blades.

The young Mexican who had placed himself in charge studied them, the reach of his fireplace poker equaling the length of the bedpost in John Kirk's hands. The other two men seemed ready to jam the knives into anyone who approached the doorway.

The one with the poker let his hot gaze settle on Mitch Kadeen. "*El jefe?*"

Mitch looked puzzled. "Heavy?"

"You are the Beeg Boss?" Che translated.

Mitch nodded. "These are my people. And this is our space." He eyed the younger man, and Teo noted the desire for revenge on the cocky little bastard on his face.

"Well *this*—" The young man gestured at the kitchen. *"This* is now our space! We will keep the food and water for ourselves before you kill us." He glared at John Kirk.

The big man, what was his name? Rafael. He spoke to Inez quietly, urging her, apparently, to escape while the others were distracted. But she was riveted by the power struggle.

Teo stepped toward the window, pitching his voice to carry, as though he were arguing before the Superior Court, with its panel benched high above the courtroom. "There is food and water enough for all. And medicine, bandages, and warm blankets." He looked from Mitch to the three angry Mexicans. "A place to sleep, to recover until the storm passes us by."

"Men like you will never let men like us live," the young man said, the poker wavering as he and the two men with him retreated through the kitchen doorway to a more defensible position. "We have to make our own way." He turned to Mitch. "Do you have a car?"

John Kirk growled. "Now you want to steal our car? What kind of lowlifes are—"

"No!" Teo interjected firmly, cutting off Mitch's response and earning an angry glare in return. *Common sense. We're not enemies. We're not. Working together will save lives. Why can't he see that?* "We don't have a car. We were dropped off here. The caretaker may have a vehicle. Since you may have killed him already…." He trailed off as Inez gasped.

"Teo, shut up. That's an order!" Mitch looked about to suffer a stroke.

Che gestured. "It is no matter. We have risked everything to come here. A little more makes no difference." He sent the other two men out the back, perhaps to search for a car, though Teo's Spanish was limited. They lumbered out in clothing that was still wet. The young Mexican glanced behind him at the woman. Rafael pulled her out of the way, ready to shove her to safety whether she wanted to go or not.

"Three days. That's all we've got to live together," Teo said. "Can't we do that? We could divide the food—"

The young Mexican growled and slammed the poker into the counter again, swung it sideways, knocking a pile of glassware onto the floor. "Shut up. Shut up! How do you Americans think, talk talk talk *talk!*" He swayed on his feet, fell back into the counter, about to drop.

Will started into the kitchen, but Mitch grabbed his arm and yanked him back.

"God damn it, just stop, all of you!" Mitch said. "Let's stop talking. Let's just take a minute. *Uno minuto.*" The senior partner appeared unsure of his words, but held his empty hands up in a clear message. "Take a seat, John, Will."

He jerked his head toward the open lounge, then looked at Teo, saw Judy finally. "Everyone. Let's just take a minute. Sit down."

Moving dreamlike, the legal team retreated toward the window. The Mexican, now braced against the counter, held the poker tight. Teo gave Rafael and Inez a reassuring smile and crossed to the fireplace, where embers still burned.

"I'm going to build the fire. We're going to need the heat," he said. When no one responded, he squatted, opened the glass and set in several small chipped sticks, along with some wadded up paper. As the flame flickered, he stacked some heavier logs atop them, pulling his sweater sleeve down when he noticed it had slid up high enough to show a discolored bruise on his forearm. Lesions. He'd become very fond of long sleeves since the diagnosis. Glancing around, he saw everyone's attention on the kitchen. *Thank heaven for drama*, he thought as he closed the doors again.

A real Mexican standoff.

Who would start the shooting?

* * * * *

CHAPTER 29

Davi Pilar watched the scene inside the *casa* through fogged binoculars, fortunate the clothing he wore was gray and not black, keeping him hidden in the blowing snow. He'd had the sense to dress warmly before he left, and he'd stolen additional clothes from the bodies dead in the snow, so he wasn't too uncomfortable.

His rifle was slung over his shoulder, handgun in his pocket. He was a hunter. His prey was nearly in his sights.

It disappointed him that perhaps only five remained alive of those who had traveled with the fat man. And none of the money.

He'd frantically searched the cab of the crashed truck, the faded cold smell of the dead men who had only one hundred American dollars in their pockets. He had taken it, of course.

And their cigarettes.

These things will kill you, man, he'd said, trying not to touch the fat man's white skin. He'd laughed at his own joke. Someone had to, and those dead Mexicans weren't in a laughing mood.

In the *casa*, the men exchanged angry words. Those he'd come to fetch had a bit more spirit left in them than Davi would have liked. That young one, the one with the fireplace poker, Davi wouldn't have much use for him at all. Too cocky by far.

But he'd received the surprise he was promised.

Inez.

He hadn't been sure at first that it was her. She looked tired, older than he remembered. The years hadn't been kind to her. But he recalled everything about her. The way she walked. The perfume she wore. The sound of her voice. Her words, those words that cut and twisted and sprayed salt on his open wounds.

Feeling that old anger boil again, he stared, hoping she'd suffered in the cold and snow. But she looked content enough. Her attention was shared between two men, the heavy-set older one and the hot-tempered young screamer. Leading them on, the way she'd led him, no doubt, waiting to see who came out on top.

Well, Davi knew who'd come out on top.

He would.

He had no choice, with the loan sharks nibbling at the back of his mind. But how to get at his quarry with a room full of people, armed as most of them were?

None were as well armed as he, of course. Some had knives, one had a poker. Looked like one of the *yanquis* had a heavy stick or something, he couldn't really make it out. The rest could have had more. Taking them all at once was risky.

The mouthy kid barked something at two of his *compadres*, the men with their shiny knives, and they vanished into a hallway. A few moments later, they slammed out through a back door and slogged toward an outbuilding. That was his opening. He'd take them down one by one if he had to, till he'd gotten what he came for.

After a final glance at the degenerating scene inside, he inched along the building, using its sandy wall to shelter him from the wind and snow. He tracked the two men, sliding his gloved hand into his pocket, almost caressing the .38 snubnose he kept in there safe from the weather.

These two were his.

Away from the hothead, perhaps he could keep them.

Two of the six or more human animals who were his. He'd only counted five, but there could be more. At two hundred apiece that was one thousand out of the ten he'd been promised; but it might justify this journey through a frozen hell. Maybe enough to pacify the sharks, for a few days.

Since the money wasn't in the truck, the *pollos* must still have it. They'd pay him now. He'd see to that.

The fools laughed and stumbled across the yard, yelling at each other over the wind. As they disappeared inside the large shed or barn, Davi ducked and ran raggedly up behind them, hiding for a moment before leaping out into the open door of the garage, gun in his hand.

Instead of noticing him, they drooled over a late model red Ford pickup truck parked to the far right. A workbench full of tools sat in the back, with a neatly arranged rack of implements on the left-hand wall. The floor was finished concrete—the first time his feet had been on something dry in ten hours. He slammed the door behind him, letting the wind howl outside.

The two men spun to gape at him, knives in their hands.

"Drop the knives!" He fired a round into the ceiling of the building. "*Ahora!*"

Uncertain, they tottered a moment. They wore jackets that were dry but too small, brightly colored and festive. Their shoes, dark and wet, looked like they'd been that way before the brief trip from the casita here, and then the taller one tossed his knife onto the floor. The other shoved at his friend, blinking in confusion. "What are you doing? Are you crazy?"

Davi tried to guess what was wrong with them. They were slow, awkward. Were they damaged? Or drunk?

He realized belatedly that was the answer. Idiots. He rushed them, and they tripped over each other, trying to escape. Grabbing the front of their thin jackets, he cracked their heads together, knocking them out. He dropped them on the floor, then took off his gloves.

His bare hands told him there was at least minimal heat here, enough to leave them safely. Davi hooked a circle of rope off the wall and tied the two men back-to-back on the floor behind the truck where they wouldn't be easily seen from the door—just in case the chili pepper boy came looking for them.

Two of his people down, three or more to go. And maybe a couple of those fancy women. Just for himself.

Davi smirked, thinking of the money, and of the good time he'd have. He stole a pair of dry gloves from the workbench and headed back to watch and wait.

* * * * *

CHAPTER 30

Jake trod lightly in his heavy work boots, praying he'd get to the office undetected. He'd heard the others moving, heard the yelling start in the kitchen again. He had to do something, take care of his people. Or he wouldn't have guests, but bodies.

The feel of the pills still jangled the nerves in his hands. He wished the girl had never brought that poison here; just knowing it existed so close drove him to the edge. He badly wanted to give John White Horse a call.

But the phones weren't working anyway. For now, others in immediate danger rated a higher priority of help than his own. That was enough motivation, as long as he kept focus.

All the same, he hoped the kid managed to get the pretty girl some help. She could still have a bright future without the anchor of an addiction dragging her down.

The warm brass of the office door handle turned smoothly in his hand as he slipped inside, closed and locked it behind him. A quick survey assured him that this space, at least, hadn't been invaded by either side.

He bent slightly to get a good look out the window. *Looks like it's letting up.* Trying to remember the forecast, he recalled it was only supposed to be bad for a day or so before the turnaround and warm-up. Could they hold on that long? He wasn't any more sure than that Teo fellow.

People could be counted on to do the exact wrong thing. It was their nature. Himself, a case in point.

As he moved across to the desk, and took a seat in the worn maroon wheeled office chair in front of the radio, the pain simmered in his back. He lusted again after a handful of the Oxys, his hand trembling as he plugged in the mike.

Here goes nothing.

"Breaker 1-9. Breaker 1-9. This is the Sherman Ranch for the District Seven State Police Barracks. Anyone out there?"

Jake waited several seconds as static crackled and repeated his request. He tried to speak loud enough for the officer to hear, but prayed like hell that the layer of dark wood paneling on the walls blocked the sound from the kitchen.

A male voice broke through the static intermittently. "District Sev— Trooper Jo—Gemail. What's y—mergency?"

With a sigh of relief, Jake held the microphone close, hoping the man heard more of what he was saying than Jake was picking up. "Listen, we're in a bad way. There's a truckload of illegals broke into the casita out here at the Sherman Ranch. They're holding my guests hostage. Any way you fellows can send someone?"

"S—Again?"

Jake muttered. "Shooting. Dead people. Illegals. Savvy?"

"Who's this?"

"Jake Patrin, caretaker for the Sherman Ranch. We've got a situation here, and someone's gonna end up dead—"

"Situation? Yeah, everyone's snowbound, all right. We're backed u— and we'll put you on the l—Soonest." His last words dissolved into prickly static.

"Hello? Hello? Come back?" Jake knocked on the microphone, frustrated, but got no further response.

"Damn it all!" *Cops got no problem being underfoot if you were hauling a few pounds over your limit or driving a little fast when there was no one else for miles on the night highway. But when you needed one?* "Cut me a friggen break."

He set the mike down, went to roll his shoulder to relieve the cramping and gasped from the wave of pain it caused.

Okay, not that. Don't move. Don't move.

He breathed through the pain, picturing the soft green fields of his Indiana homelands, the one his physical therapist had created for his escape. Visualization, she'd called it. Load of hooey, he'd called it, till he'd got the thing down, made it his own. It did work. Sometimes.

Green fields, corn knee high by the Fourth of July. Blue skies. Gentle breeze. Feel it on your face, the warm sun, the tickle of breeze. Breathe. Breathe.

He didn't know how long he could stand the pain. Teo was right. He'd really been hurt when the Mexicans attacked him, something serious. But he had guests. He had business. And he remembered something to help him take care of it.

In the office closet was a pair of Remington shotguns and a box of shells. Strictly defense as far as he was concerned. He'd never shot more with them than a couple rocks, trying to scare off a coyote too close to the house.

But no one else had a gun; that made Jake king of the hill. Maybe he could get their attention long enough to break the impasse.

Shoving himself to his feet, he limped to the dark stained wooden door and pulled it open. The double-barreled model sat ready and waiting. Balancing it on his knee, he cracked it open. Tearing the lid off the box of shells with his right hand, he shoved two into the chamber before snapping the barrel back into place.

"If we can't count on the staties, we'll have to handle it ourselves. Maybe they'll make it here in time to clean up the debris," he mused aloud, allowing the self-mockery to permeate his tone.

So what did that make him? Underdog to the rescue? Mighty Mouse? Rocky the Raccoon?

But instead of the superhero, the Beatles tune came to mind. He smirked at the irony, and let the song bring lightness to the moment he found filled with dread.

* * * * *

CHAPTER 31

Inez shivered, still not feeling herself, the current situation beyond her experience. She hadn't dealt much with Americans, other than bright-shirted tourists visiting her town. What a spread of personalities they shared.

The one who was the leader, silver-haired and commanding, and the loud muscular one made a huge presence in the room. She'd known men like that, men of power, they believed they could do what they chose, that they were entitled. A doctor at the hospital where she studied had come on to many of the women. Not Inez, because she made herself unattractive, mussing her hair, not looking him in the eye. She didn't trust them, Mexican or Yanqui.

The woman with glasses, Judy, was different. And the men who had taken them to the water, as painful as that had been. They huddled by the fireplace, as afraid as she.

Che still held the hard black metal stick, waved it, threatening. He'd left ugly dark gouges in the countertop and the closet door where he'd struck them. He'd taken down one man. How long before he'd kill?

All the things she wanted to say were trapped in her mouth. The warm, flirty feelings she'd played at faded like wood smoke as she discovered this violent, filthy side of his nature. He was like other hot-blooded young men, relying on bravado and street smarts to scrape by. There was no future for young men like that.

Not with her, anyway.

Rafael was right. They had nothing else to gain here. If Rai and Trini found a truck that could navigate the roads in this frozen land, they could get away from here before anyone died.

Even if they escaped this disaster, where would they go? At least under the control of the coyotes, there had been a plan. They would be transferred to the new driver, go on to St. Louis, and blend into the community. Now? Inez had no more idea how to get to St. Louis than to the moon.

"What shall we do?" she whispered to Rafael.

"He cannot go on for much longer. None of us can. We need sleep.

We need someplace safe." Rafael sighed. "Since he has poisoned the others against us, we won't be safe here. If we were to lay down now, something bad would happen. This I know." He pulled a stool closer for her. "You should sit."

Inez shook her head. Her feet hurt, ached. Her eyes burned with fatigue. She'd lost track how long it had been since they left Juarez, first in the black, close darkness, then the blinding white cold. Here, the drugs had expanded her sense of time so she couldn't tell. The clock said it was las tres, three o'clock, and it wasn't dark, so it must be the afternoon.

But what day?

They'd left Juarez on Monday. Was it Tuesday? Wednesday? Later? She had no idea.

After a final angry exchange, Che moved back into the kitchen. The Americans backed away. Everyone seemed determined to calm down. She tried to keep any challenge from her eyes as she watched Che, but he flared anyway, grabbing her arm.

"What do you want, Inez?" he growled. "Shall I be an eager puppy, barking only to please my new master? If I did not stand up for us, they would kill me."

Rafael pulled her away. "Che, think. They have no reason to kill you, except perhaps that you are acting like a madman. It is no different than in the truck. You are a firecracker." He snapped his fingers. "All noise and fizzled in five minutes. You have to think. You have to be calm."

Che stumbled and swung the metal stick at Rafael. Inez could stand it no further. She stepped around Rafael and grabbed Che's arm, yanking it hard, letting her pain and frustration pour out onto him.

"You must to stop this. We'll all end up dead. Is that the future we all wanted in America? We came here to make our lives better, to make something of ourselves, to survive somewhere beyond the gutter. Look at yourself. You've done nothing."

She shook him for a shocked few moments before his eyes blazed, and he reacted. He backhanded her, then shoved her into the counter. She hit the hard edge with her ribs, gasping with pain.

Rafael yelled, but Che whirled on him again, stick raised.

Then two gunshots rang out, echoing in the small space, and Inez hit the floor.

* * * * *

CHAPTER 32

Jake Patrin strolled into the kitchen, aware of shocked looks from both sides of the pass-through. The woman Inez lay on the floor in the middle of the kitchen. He verified the two holes in the ceiling just above the barely-smoking barrel of his weapon. He hadn't hit her.

"Now look here. I'm putting an end to all this foolishness," Jake said, addressing Che but clearly encompassing the Artotech faction as well. He caught a glimpse of his reflection in the window, saw he looked as washed out as he felt.

"There is goddamn well enough space and enough food and enough beds here for everyone for the next two days. No sense in this violence carrying on. Put the goddamn stick down." He fixed Che with a cold glare.

To his right, Rafael bent down to check Inez.

"She all right, *amigo*?" Jake asked.

Rafael shook the slight woman, sighed as she responded by grasping his hand and coming to her feet. "She is very tired. We all are."

"Damn straight, chief. We're all damn tired of this." Jake slid two more shells into his shotgun, closed it with a loud click, and took a step closer to Che. "Now you and me, we got some business. I wouldn't mind shooting your ass for what you've done, but that won't solve a damn thing. Unless you don't put down that poker. You got three seconds to do it, or I'll drop you where you stand. And I ain't kidding."

Rafael moved aside with Inez, leaving Jake plenty of room.

A flutter of pastels caught his attention across the passthrough as Annike and Cattrin stumbled belatedly into the scene.

"What's happened? Mitch? Who's shot?" Annike's shocked face appeared in the doorway, paling even further as she saw the gun.

The interruption distracted Che, too, and Jake took advantage of it.

"Now!" Jake barked, and the poker dropped to the floor, Che crumpling up into the corner of the kitchen cabinets. Rafael ducked under the barrel of the gun to grab the metal poker, and tossed it through the doorway behind him into the back hall.

Mitch stepped up and pulled the women into the lounge behind him, turning their agitated questioning over to John Kirk. Then he stepped into the kitchen. "What do you need?"

Jake looked around the kitchen. "First off, we got to find the other two. Someone should check on the woman down the hall." He watched as Rafael and Will dragged a half-conscious Che into the other room to secure him in a chair with some bungee cords the trainers had left on a table for the next day's exercises. The Artotech lawyers immediately began a buzzing debate on consequences.

Jake took anything that even remotely looked like a weapon and tossed it in a cupboard. "All right. Now...." His back nearly vibrated with pain, the waves coming with any small movement. He had to keep going, stay focused.

His gaze sought out Will. "How's your little friend? She gonna be all right?"

Will nodded. "Yeah. She's sleeping—probably better off that way. How are you doing?" Will came into the kitchen, and looked at Jake's back. Across the shoulders of his flannel shirt was a dark splash of blood from the attack. He winced. "Doesn't look good."

Jake gave a faint smile, used the shotgun as a makeshift cane, leaning heavily on it. "Not as bad as getting hit by a truck." He sighed tiredly. "Someone put a pot of coffee on? And get some more food out. It's gonna be a long night."

Judy came to do as he asked, Will helping her. The Mexican woman joined them, starting to clean up the mess the young man had made.

Jake eyed the big Mexican. "Hey, Ralph, where's your buddies?"

Rafael glanced out the window, then down the hall. "They go look for car."

He frowned. "Where do they think they're gonna go in this snow anyway?"

The other man looked a little lost, and Jake waved him into the kitchen. "Come get something to eat, all of you. How long they been out there anyway, Ralph?"

The big man frowned. *"Una hora, quizá más."*

"An hour? It ain't that far." Puzzled, Jake craned his head to look out the kitchen window toward the shed, groaned. "It's at least closed in, and it's got heat. So it's not an emergency, I guess. It can wait."

What about the rest of the flock? Teo sat on the window seat, distancing himself from the bickering attorneys and the one Inez had called Che. Jake inched carefully around the room, checking the fireplace and the windows, wishing like hell the aspirin would kick in.

Will and Inez brought plates out to the lounge. "I'm worried about you," Will confessed, frowning as Jake passed him. "You need medical care."

"When the staties get here, we'll all get what we need, son. Just waiting on that."

"What will they do?" Will asked. "Turn these people over to immigration? Send them back to an economically disadvantaged country when they're willing to risk their lives for a chance to make something of themselves? After what they've been through the past couple of days, I'd say they'd earned the right to stay."

Mitch frowned from across the room. "That's not your call, Starlin. I understand your feelings for the rights of these people, but the fact is they're not citizens, they didn't belong here in the first place." He glared at Che. "And that one's facing criminal charges, if I've got anything to say about it."

Annike nodded. "Those who haven't been involved in the criminal activity won't be in any trouble," she said softly, as if that might reassure Rafael and Inez.

As if it would, Jake thought. *As if returning to a life hard enough to drive them into the dark on a truck with a man who's likely extorted hundreds or thousands of dollars in the sheer hope of something better would reassure them.*

Mitch straightened his shoulders, walked over for a cup of coffee from Judy. "Frankly, I'm all for scrapping this whole experiment as soon as the phone lines open. We're out of here."

"This never happened at the Ritz-Carlton," Cattrin puffed.

Will shot her a look. "Well, it happens a lot of places around the country, Ms. Odeon. We're fortunate to have a high standard of living compared to the rest of the world. Three billion people in the world live on less each day than you spend for a cup of Starbucks on the way to the office." He was taut with outrage. "How dare you reduce their struggle to an inconvenience!"

"See here, you little bleeding heart—"

Mitch cut off the attack with a hand on Cattrin's arm. "Enough. We'll get nowhere fighting among ourselves."

"Now that's the smartest thing I've heard all day." Jake grimaced and walked back to the kitchen to check on the food preparation.

Teo laughed softly, winked at Will. "See? All that hard work over the last four days and all you had to do was arrange an invasion."

Will sighed and took a seat in a chair near the window. "I think it's our company motto. We won't give up until someone's thoroughly convinced, or dead. How's that for determination?

Mitch herded the rest to the kitchen. The women twittered about steps to take, punishments to deal out.

Jake just shook his head, glad he only had to deal with these people for seven days. He'd never have been able to work with them full time. *Never.*

He escaped to the lounge, meaning to share some insight with the young Harmonics trainer, but his eye was drawn past Teo out the window. The snow had stopped. A dark figure, stark against the tapestry of white, was plunging toward the building with what looked like a gun in hand. Shocked, he missed a beat. "Everybody down! Now!"

Jake sensed reaction all around him as people ducked for cover, but Teo was caught in the center of the room. He turned to face the window as the pane blew inward in a thousand pieces or more. More bullets knocked Teo to the floor as the dark figure jumped through the open window.

"Give me my people and I might let you live!" the rough-voiced man announced where he stood on the window seat. Swathed in scarf and coats, his face was barely visible.

Jake started to swing his shotgun into play, but the man took aim across the room, where Will and Inez crouched in easy range. "Drop it, my man. I'll shoot them all. I don't care."

Torn, Jake hesitated, then he bent painfully and set the gun on the floor in front of him. He stared down at Teo, bleeding silently into the rug, his face pale. He had splinters of the glass stuck into him, everywhere, and at least one shot in the shoulder. Feeling sick, Jake wondered how the day could have possibly gotten even worse.

Would any of them make it out alive?

* * *

Teo picked up the shock on Jake's face before the words sunk in. Something bad was happening. In slow motion, he turned, caught a blurred glimpse of a moving person, then the world exploded.

He felt a shatter of pinpricks across the front of his shirt, hardly had time to look down to confirm the injuries, the trickle of blood *his blood* that came from each before he felt like he'd been punched in the shoulder, knocked back flat to the ground.

Hurt hurt hurt

The man came through the open window with a blast of frigid air, onto the terra cotta pillow where Teo had been sitting a moment before.

The pain drew him back to the moment, seconds passing like shutter flashes, bright with sharp edges as he lay on his back on the nubbly rug.

There was shouting around him, the man yelling. It was dark—No, his eyes were closed. He fought to open them, but only caught glimpses of what was going on.

The man jumped down from the ledge with a heavy thud and stalked past him. Who was it? He'd thought the Mexicans were all together. What had the man demanded? His "people?" What was that about?

Teo's thoughts drifted off, and the man with the gun became a king on a throne, the weapon morphing to a long, polished scepter as he waved it, dictating futures of the gathered. The shouting continued in a fog, and the man became Moses, pleading with the Pharaoh to let his people go. Staccato commands in Spanish penetrated the fog, more shots.

Am I dying?

No. He couldn't be. Not after all the careful tending, the secrets, the expensive medications paid for from his own pocket so that they didn't appear on the company insurance rosters. He had a strong chance of a survival rate five years out, his doctor had assured him. *My five years….*

Teo's leg twitched. He realized he could feel his whole body. He hadn't been shot in the spine, then, wasn't paralyzed. There was hope. He forced his eyes open, looked over to Inez, frozen behind the chair next to the fireplace. She stared at him, helpless. Will's body was interposed between her and the kitchen. *He was a good kid. Everyone needed a good man…*

It was an idle thought, one of many that were wafting through his head, alternating with the throbbing pain. He followed one thought, a particularly troubling reminder that his blood was contagious, poison, and faded into unconsciousness.

* * * * *

CHAPTER 33

Davi Pilar was disappointed when the man with the gun fired into the ceiling. He'd expected to be the only one with a gun. This new development complicated matters considerably.

He didn't like complicated. He liked easy.

The wind had steadily diminished for the last hour, and the snow had begun to die down. The situation inside was getting heated. But the young firebrand, the one Davi had been most worried about, had been neutralized. That was a blessing he hadn't expected.

The old man with the gun must be some sort of employee. Employees had responsibilities. They could be coerced into behaving a certain way for the benefit of their employers.

Once Davi had their attention.

The best offense…was going to be the best offense, he thought wryly. The picture window he'd spied through was as good an entry as any. He ran in place for half a minute, pumping his body up, shaking off the cold, then burst into a sprint for the window, shooting the glass as he approached to open the way.

It wasn't till he passed through that he saw the stricken face of the slim man who'd been standing in front of the window. Red spread across the front of his sweater and slacks as he fell. By then Davi was inside, standing on the cushioned window ledge. He swung his gun, meeting the eyes in each shocked face.

"Drop the gun, old man," he yelled at the employee. "Or I'll start with the right side and take them all down!"

The caretaker hesitated, but Davi had read him well. The old man read him, too. He knew just what Davi was, why he was there, and what was important to him.

So be it. As long as I get what's coming to me.

He jumped down and strutted across the room. The expressions on those faces showed fear. It made him feel like a big man, finally. All these self-important slugs would do what he said now. He smelled the coffee, the warm food, and realized how long he'd been out in the cold. Gun prominently displayed, he crossed to the kitchen.

He poured himself a big cup of coffee and drained half of it, letting its bitterness recharge him, his eye on the obvious "guests" in the other room. The one man still lay on the floor, the caretaker inching toward him. Davi froze him with a stare.

The big Mexican in the kitchen, one of his people, Davi tried to interrogate him. But the big man played dumb, wouldn't even look at him.

"Don't you know who I am, *amigo*? I'm your ride to St. Louis. But we got a little problem here. Your coyote, he run off with all the money. We don't have enough to get you the rest of the way. So you gonna have to get me some more."

The man continued to stare at the floor. Maybe this one was retarded or something. Davi growled. He'd counted on the Mexicans being interested in getting safely on. It wasn't like the Americans wanted them there. This should have been quick, like visiting a Mexican prostitute. Slam, bam, thank you ma'am, as the Americans said. But his people weren't gravitating to him for help.

And where was his little pigeon?

Davi scanned the room, saw Inez at last hiding behind a chair. She watched him, eyes wide, frightened. Good. Good. Now she could see what kind of man she'd spit on. The kind who took charge. The kind who got things done.

He shrugged off several layers of clothing and kicked them aside, ignoring the smell as they fell in a heap. He swaggered over to Inez. "So, *chica*, you finally left your little town for the big world, did you?"

Her voice was just as he remembered it, cool and unfeeling. "And you finally found your calling, feeding the torment of your countrymen and gouging them for money to bring them here." Her eyes burned, not with passion, but with hatred.

He tried not to snap-react, but it was hard. Back in Mexico, he could have slapped her into silence. "Sweet Inez. Fate brought us together, you know."

"You've just murdered a man. Forgive me if that doesn't commend your character!" She stood up, knees wavering. She tried to avoid him to check the man on the floor.

He brought the gun to bear on her. "Stay where you are."

She raised an eyebrow. "You'd shoot me rather than let me save him? *Follacabras.* You never change, Davi Pilar."

Davi froze as she called him the worst kind of sexual deviant. He was losing control of the situation. He had to do something, and quickly. His head fogged up, probably an after-product of the cold and his exhaustion.

Think, damn it, think. He bought time while he studied the people around him, paranoid about signs of threat. There were so many of them and one of him.

What could he do?

Now he had them, what would he do with them?

The coyote's original truck would go nowhere. His own truck was likely still battery-dead. That left the red pickup in the barn.

"Does that truck run? The one outside in the shed?" he asked the old man.

"I don't know. Seems to me, nothing will run on the roads today, friend." His smile was empty, like a drained tequila bottle. His gaze flicked to the gun he'd tossed on the floor, lying there so close but so far.

Davi took two steps forward and kicked the gun out of reach, out into the kitchen.

"Then we will wait."

He glanced down at the man on the floor, Inez's words still stinging him. Annoyed, Davi rounded up the rest of the people, herding them to the far end of the room behind the fireplace. The old man lagged behind, muttering about a medical kit.

"Let me keep you from being a murderer," he said. "We can save him."

Davi shrugged. "Don't get any ideas, *Americano*. If you come back with another gun, I'll shoot everyone in this house."

The old man gave him a sharp nod and limped out. The others watched him go, their hungry eyes hoping for some magical device or quick trick to save them all.

Ha! No magic will save you all now. I have the power. Do you see this, Inez? I control life and death!

So the man was dead...or dying.

Now what was he gonna do about that? One of the rich men was shot, might die. So even if Davi left here with his cargo, the *polizia* would be looking for him, wouldn't they? Soon as the snow let up.

If they discovered what happened.

If anyone could tell them what happened.

So I can't leave anyone behind alive.

The enormity of such a plan slowed even Davi Pilar for a few moments. There were what, seven? Eight? Maybe more he didn't know about? And if by chance they had managed to get a description out, they'd still be looking for him, unless....

What if there was a shootout here? A bunch of Mexicans, a bunch of Americans—and they all ended up dead? Cops would show up and assume they'd killed each other, right?

The idea grew on him, especially as he thought of all the Mexicans out in the truck, already dead, but preserved by the cold. If they dragged half a dozen of them inside, then he could shoot them, shoot the Americans and leave it all for the history books while he took his people out.

And if "his people" gave him any trouble? They could join the pile.

Davi smiled, starting to like this plan. Inez would have to go with him, then. She'd want to. She'd see how powerful he was. He could win her, if he'd persevere.

How would he get the bodies in here? No way he could do it himself, not and maintain control. He had to force the men to do it for him. He'd hold the women here until they came back.

"All the American women, over here!" he barked, gesturing to the far corner of the room.

"Now listen here, you—" the boss man protested, but Davi cocked his gun and he was still.

"Now." Davi inched his way to the blinds, ripped the cords down. He kicked several of the smaller chairs together. "Come sit down, ladies. This is *not* an invitation."

He fired the gun into the ceiling over the little dark haired one's head, and tile rained down around her. "You won't be harmed as long as the others do just what they're told."

The American women didn't move. *Putas.*

With a roar of anger, he crossed the room and grabbed the tall blonde who stared in disbelief. He dragged her to the chairs, tied her arm to the chair arm. "The rest of you have exactly three seconds to start moving or I'll shoot this one." He held the weapon to the blonde American's head.

"Oh my God!" squealed the tiny dark-skinned one. He wasn't sure if she was American, other than she was decidedly in the camp of the rich. She dressed better than anyone who might have been his cargo. But her dark skin and eyes made him wonder. He pinned her with his hot gaze and she walked over quickly, took a seat next to the blonde. The woman with glasses followed, then, leaving just Inez on her knees by the fallen man. He finished tying them.

The men watched, helpless.

But he had the power. And the gun.

Once they were tightly secured, Davi walked to the sink, poured a glass of cold water and carried it into the other room, threw it on the little hot-tempered *cholo*. The young man's eyes flipped open and he sputtered, choking.

"What is —who the fuck are you?" the kid howled. He struggled with the cords, looked around at the others.

"I am your salvation," Davi smirked. He explained quickly in Spanish that he was giving the orders. He would get them to St. Louis as promised, but a few matters must be set straight before they left. He spoke loud enough so Inez could hear him, though she steadfastly ignored him.

"You have a stake in making sure we get away from here clean," he warned her. "If you do not want to deal with *la migra*, you will do as I say."

She continued to ignore him.

Disgusted, he turned to the other men. The boss man, and the guy with the broad shoulders watched him intently.

"You're taking a trip, *caballeros*. You'll go out to the truck and pick up some of my friends, and bring them in. They'll thaw, I'm sure. Three should be enough."

He approved of the growing expressions of horror on their faces.

"I'll give you an hour," he said. "Then I start shooting the women."

* * * * *

CHAPTER 34

Inez felt as frozen as she'd been in the snow, while Davi Pilar ordered them all about as if he was worth something.

On the journey, she'd envisioned possible encounters between herself and Davi, once they'd met again. She'd flattered herself he might try to be kind, hoping to rekindle a flame long turned to ash. She'd wondered if he'd treat her as a stranger, punishing her for her rejection. She'd imagined many other scenes inbetween.

But never this.

He did recognize her, though. He'd seemed to be looking for her. Perhaps one of the coyotes had warned him she was on the truck.

It was the kind of joke men would enjoy.

He walked over to her, a cruel smile on his face. The clothing he'd discarded reeked of body odor and so did he. She turned away in disgust as he taunted her about leaving her little town.

When she didn't respond, Davi drew back as if she'd slapped him. Had he thought she'd find him attractive now that he was a *norteño*? Is this the model that Mexican men now held as a standard? She glanced over at Che, remembering how he'd strutted and threatened, an early version of what stood before her.

She set her mind on helping the injured man, and evaluated him as she'd been taught at the hospital. Blood trickled from more places than she'd ever seen before. His breathing was ragged and his pulse fast. He would only bleed more. It had to be stopped.

Something nagged her about the calculating look on Davi's face. She'd seen that look before, when he watched her at the hospital. He was considering a plan—a plan that had bad elements. What was he up to?

Moments later, he started yelling at the Americans, tied the women up in chairs at the far end of the room while their men did nothing. Scanning their faces, she saw they'd realized the tables had turned. When she and the others had arrived, they'd been terrified about how the gringos would treat them. Now it was their turn to see how an expatriate Mexican would deal with them. Sadly, there didn't seem to be much difference. Except Davi was prepared to kill.

She couldn't see Rafael, but thought he remained in the kitchen. She looked around at the men, saw Che was still unconscious. Trini and Raimundo had never returned from their trip outside—what had happened to them? For a moment she regretted Che's descent into unconsciousness. At least he'd had the spirit to challenge their circumstances.

Davi stalked over to the sleeping Che, woke him with a splash of water. Gun in hand, he then laid out his plan to have the men, Che and Rafael included, go out to the truck and gather dead bodies to bring to the house.

Horrified, Inez could only stare at him. What could his purpose be? Certainly he was not seeking a proper Christian burial for those poor lost souls. What would he need those bodies for?

As Che failed to respond, Davi threatened to shoot the American women if the men did not return quickly enough. Then the little dark woman he'd tied up started screaming.

* * * * *

CHAPTER 35

Some days you just can't get a goddamn break.

Jake had surrendered the shotgun at the intruder's demand, well aware there were too many potential targets. Where had this bastard come from?

Had he been hanging around outside, waiting for the hothead to take control? Based on the condition of those who'd come in from the cold, he couldn't believe this was just another one.

My people, he'd said.

His people?

Sudden realization hit Jake like that long-ago truck. This man must be the local *coyote*, the one Ralph thought was dead. So, what motivated him was money. And he would only get money if his "cargo" was alive and uninjured.

That was one mark on their side of the tote board. He wouldn't kill anyone worth cash.

The *coyote* jumped down, stepped over Teo and walked heavily toward the kitchen, reloading the pistol with the ease of much practice. He eyeballed Rafael, spitting out demands in Spanish. Rafael didn't respond, kept his gaze focused on the ground.

Annike laid a manicured hand on Jake's arm. "Is that another one of them?" she whispered, shivering, her pale skin even whiter.

"No," he said softly. "That's one of the men transporting the folk north for the money. He needs them alive to make it worth his while."

Kadeen, standing behind her, eyed the man in the kitchen. "*Them*," was all he said.

"That's right, *Americano*. 'Them.'" The man stared darkly back from the kitchen. "You, I have no need for. Except maybe one of your pretty pretties."

Kadeen stiffened. John Kirk sneered. "Over my dead body."

Jake shook his head, realizing what the big man must not—that having shot one of the lawyers already, the *coyote* had nothing left to lose. *Too many movies, that one.* He probably intended to kill more of them, certainly anyone who stood in his way.

"We don't want your people," Kadeen said. "We're just renting this place for a week. We didn't let them in, we didn't ask them to come. If you've got business with them, take them and go." He stood a little taller, Jake thought, as he moved into a more comfortable mode. One lion to another.

"Then we understand each other." He went for some hot coffee, and Jake took the opportunity to take a few steps back, giving himself a little more room to do—what? The *coyote* still had the upper hand.

But he might be able to be distracted. "Where are the others?" Jake asked casually.

The man ignored his question and jerked his head toward the garage. "Does that truck run?"

"Seems to me, nothing will run on the roads today."

The man shrugged. "Then we will wait. "

"Teo can't wait!" Will burst in from the next room. "He needs help now!"

The man twitched, apparently realizing he'd left his back open. "All of you, in the other room." He pointed the gun at them, gestured as they started to move. Kadeen stepped forward, let the three women pass behind him, blocking the *coyote*'s access to them.

"Where's a medical kit?" Will called from the lounge by the fireplace.

"There's one behind the pantry here," Jake said. He looked at the *coyote*. "It okay with you if I grab some bandaids, chief? In case we can save the man before he dies."

The man hesitated, his gaze wavering a moment along with the point of his gun barrel. "Yeah, yeah whatever," he said finally, shoving Kadeen after his women. "For all the good it will do."

Jake crossed to the back entry to the kitchen, wondering if he'd be able to sneak down the hall for the other gun. The way he was moving, he doubted it. The injury site had swollen so much, leaving twinges of nerve pain and numbness. He might not even be able to remain upright for much longer. *Damn that kid. Better not risk it.*

He got the kit and returned across the room, passing by the *coyote*. He handed Inez a stack of maxipads, then set the kit down on the floor. Teo, pale and still bleeding, lay very still, unconscious. A quick hand on his chest let Jake know he still breathed.

"He need doctor," Inez whispered. Her thin fingers trembled as she waited for his instructions.

He tried to sound confident enough for both of them. "Well, we'll do the best we can, okay, hon?"

She didn't look like she understood his words, but after a moment, she returned his smile.

The gunman started barking orders, dragging Jake's attention from his work. He started ordering the women around, had them tied up at gunpoint.

Jake's moral center rebelled against his guests being treated so poorly, but he was in no shape to take any action. The Artotech men could have done something, but they moved like sheep, in shock. All Jake could do was take care of the man on the floor.

The Mexican woke Che, and started yelling in Spanish. Jake had enough Spanish to know he was promising them their trip to St. Louis. He wanted Che to help him do something, and he drafted the other men, too, ordering them to retrieve the bodies from outside.

What could the bastard be thinking? The man continued in muttered Spanish, provoking shocked looks from Che and Inez. *Crap. Something bad.*

"No. You can't do that."

The cry came from the confined women, the one called Cattrin. She stared at the *coyote* in revulsion, then turned to Kadeen.

"He means to kill us when you leave!" she shrieked. "Don't do what he says!"

The *coyote* froze, spun around. "I knew you were one of mine."

He stalked across the room and slapped her hard, twice. "*Puta!* I'll teach you to lie to me!" he said in Spanish. "Pretending you're one of these fine people when you're nothing but a cow?"

As all the women screamed and tried to scoot away from him, he cut the line and dragged Cattrin away from them by her hair, tossing her across to stand with Che. "You stay. I'll deal with you when I've sent these men off." His dark look was deep with foreboding.

Jake got to his feet, driven to intervene somehow, though he wasn't sure what he'd do. Kadeen and the others had scattered during the fracas. The Mexican noticed, too, and started for the kitchen. But he never got there.

What faced him was the previously docile Rafael, holding Jake's shotgun, his expression determined. He aimed and dropped a double load of shot into the *coyote*'s face and chest.

Disbelief written on his face, the coyote dropped his gun, following it to the floor.

"*No mas. No mas,*" Rafael whispered tiredly. The gun slipped from his fingers and the big man began to sob.

* * * * *

CHAPTER 36

In the stunned silence that followed the shots, Jake went back to Teo, took a deep breath and checked for a pulse. It was there, faint but there. He stared down at the multiple red flowers of blood, able to see his breath in the chill air.

"Okay, it's A, B, C," he said. "First check the airway, then breathing, then circulation." Jake groaned as he reached across Teo's body for the kit. "The worst of the bleeding looks like it's stopped—"

He broke off when Teo reached for his hand and shoved it away.

"Don't touch me," Teo whispered through pale lips.

Will came up to help. "It's okay, Teo, he's got first aid training. Everything's under control."

"No." The word was firm. "Don't touch me."

"Come on now, pal, you've got a few issues. We can patch you up pretty well." Jake surveyed the extent of the damage. "I think it just needs cleaned up." He ripped open several packages of 4 by 4 gauze and grabbed a bottle of peroxide. "Might sting a bit, though. Especially getting some of that glass out. Want a bullet to bite?" he added, trying to make light.

Teo fought his eyes open and grabbed Jake's wrist, holding him away. "No one can touch me. Contamination." His pain-filled gaze probed Jake's face, moved to Will's. "Please."

Confounded, Jake glanced around at the rest of the lawyers. Post-trauma, the blonde was in in tears, the boss with his arm around her shoulder. Judy had gone to the kitchen, comforting Ralph, getting him something to drink. John Kirk paced like someone lost in the forest.

None of them had gone to help Cattrin, sitting, near-catatonic, just where the man had left her. Inez must have noticed her condition, while their patient refused treatment. She moved over next to the woman, smoothed her hair, speaking to her softly in Spanish.

Well now. Look at that. It might have been funny if the whole scene wasn't so tragic.

What was he going to do about Teo?

"You got to up front this one, partner," Jake persisted. "What's the problem? I got to get the blood off you to see what's damaged."

"He's homosexual," Annike offered from behind them.

Jake growled at her. "I don't care if he's pink, blue or Indian…." Like a flash of bright light, the import of her comment sunk in. He studied Teo. "Is that it?"

Teo nodded slowly. "Blood…"

"He's got AIDS?" John Kirk moved away, around the pass-through into the kitchen as though germs were even now wafting through the air toward him.

"AIDS?" Will looked surprised, pulled back his hand but didn't move otherwise.

"Not yet," Teo whispered, his eyes closing. "HIV positive, though. Just leave me." *Now, this is a first.* "Whoo. Well."

Jake considered his next move, but found the information didn't really change the situation. Medical professionals worked with AIDS-affected patients all the time, wearing latex gloves. As long as they didn't exchange body fluids, they would be fine. They were still people. They still needed help.

"Damned if we don't have to do this anyway." He rummaged through his kit, but didn't find what he needed. He turned to Will.

"Son, go out in the kitchen and get me some clear plastic wrap and some large sandwich bags, will you?"

Teo continued to protest. "Please, don't take the risk." He could hardly move, and each time he tried, he bled a little more.

"Goddamn it, no one's gonna die on my watch," Jake muttered. He took the packages from Will and first wrapped his hands with the clear wrap, then slid them inside the zipper bags. He eyed Mitch. "Toss me a set of pliers and a bowl from the kitchen."

Mitch only hesitated a moment before he went for the items. "Shouldn't you call a professional?"

"You got one handy?" Jake did nothing to disguise the irritation in his voice.

Mitch's face flushed, and he quickly brought the requested tool.

"Now, why don't you gentlemen get that window covered up before we all freeze? Plastic and nails are in the—" Jake closed his eyes and counted. "Third room down that hall on the left, little workshop of mine. Or if you're real ambitious, head out to the garage and get some plywood. Other two illegals are out there anyway apparently."

He'd spoken loud enough for everyone to hear, but no one moved. "Or maybe you'd rather leave the animals out in the barn."

Jake waited another minute, then shook his head. "Damn useless people."

He gave up and turned to focus on Teo. "Now listen, my friend. You've got at least one gunshot wound, maybe more." He pushed Teo's protesting hand away. "I was an Army medic, son I'm going to do this. Even if I have to knock you out. But I'd rather not do that because I've got a better gauge of your condition awake, you hear me?"

Teo murmured something, half awake.

Silence around them for a moment, then Mitch's face contorted. "All right, people, let's get the place functional again. You heard the man. Plastic and nails down the hall. Someone get a broom and sweep up the glass."

"I will help," Che volunteered. "Please. I can carry things. I—" He glanced at Cattrin, still sitting near him, devastated by the *coyote's* treatment. "I want you to see I'm not like that one, the other."

Mitch eyed him hotly for a moment, but finally Annike nodded.

"We can use all the help we can get."

Will took a cue from Mitch, slipped over to loose the bonds that held Che to the chair. Che got up, stretched, groaned. At the movement near her, Cattrin suddenly stiffened, then pulled away, retreated back along the far hall somewhere.

Inez came to help Jake, wrapping her hands as Jake had. He handed her the pliers and she used them to remove small bits of glass embedded in Teo's flesh. Jake did the most of the removal, while Will, hands protected, blotted the blood away and rinsed with hydrogen peroxide. Sometime in the process, Teo fainted.

Well, who could blame him? There had to be twenty or more of the splinters, but most were obvious and they seemed to clear and close up easily.

"Did you know?" Jake asked Judy.

The Denver partner, a bit strained after the events of the day, shook her head. "About Teo? I remember when he came out in Chicago a couple of years ago. But I had no idea he was HIV positive. I don't think anyone did. He kept it well covered." She sighed. "And this, of all things, to bring it into the open."

They worked quietly but quickly, uncovering a wound in the left shoulder where the bullet passed all the way through, and another on the left thigh where a bullet had torn through the skin but hadn't done any major damage. These were cleaned as best they could be and bandaged, covered over with plastic as well.

The others returned with a large sheet of plywood and several flats of plastic, and managed to get the window sealed up once again, Rafael and the two other Mexican men working side by side with John Kirk and Mitch. Will swept the floor clean of the remainder of the broken glass.

Judy took Annike into the kitchen, and soon good smells emanated from there, and the room started to warm up again.

When they'd done all they could for Teo, Jake carried the bowlful of glass to the kitchen, carefully depositing the whole thing in a zipped plastic bag before he set it outside. Will brought out a heavy blanket that allowed the men to carry Teo back to his room to rest more comfortably. John Kirk protested his place in the room, and Mitch told him to move his things out for Teo's sake so he wouldn't be disturbed.

Once Teo was carefully installed in bed, Judy met them in the bathroom with antiseptic wash. Those who had treated Teo peeled off the plastic, sealing that away in another plastic bag to be left outside. Then they washed their hands in steaming water with soap, doused them in clear rubbing alcohol.

"Is he going to live?" she asked Jake.

Jake shrugged from habit, then winced as the pain shot through his back. "None of the wounds were life-threatening. But...."

"Yeah." She sighed.

Jake wondered what she was thinking, but guessed it had something to do with Teo's standing at the firm. He knew from his own experience they couldn't just fire him; the Americans With Disabilities Act would block that. They might pay him off first, before it could come to that.

One decision that's not my problem. Thank God for small favors.

Once his hands were clean, Jake took a quick tour of the *casa,* seeing what needed to be done next. Annike and Judy had cleaned up the blood in the hall where the *coyote* had been shot, armed with their own heavy plastic gloves they must have found under the sink. The *coyote*'s body was nowhere to be seen. Will tossed some logs on the fire, beefing up the heat. What was left?

"I should, ah...I'll give the staties a call, see if they've got a chopper, maybe, to airlift your friend out."

Mitch looked as worn as Jake felt. He held out a conciliatory hand. "Thanks for everything you've done, Jake. If it wasn't for you, this could have turned out a lot worse. You saved our lives."

Jake shook his hand. "Wasn't only me, friend. Team effort, you know. That was the point of the thing, right? Learning to work together?"

Adrenaline starting to wear off, he didn't wait for a response, but headed back to the office, his limp more pronounced.

Zanna Michaels appeared in the hallway, hair rumpled, rubbing her eyes. "What's going on? Is that—blood—on the rug?"

"Go check with your buddy," Jake growled. "He'll fill you in."

She didn't seem to notice his irritation, just wandered off to find Will.

Jake stopped to wash his hands once more, finding them shaking a bit now that the crisis had passed. He ought to call the ranch owners and notify them of the situation, but something felt like the other shoe hadn't dropped just yet. He'd wait.

Instead he radioed the state patrol that they'd had intruders, shots had been fired, and at least one man was dead. That seemed to light a fire under them, and they promised to be out in a matter of hours.

Jake passed by his room, taking a moment to glance in at the blanketed double bed, long enough to wish he could take a few hours in there. *Pull the covers over my head, pretend the week's starting over again...sounds like heaven, huh?*

With a sigh, he tore himself away from the sight and returned to the kitchen. A spread fit for a king had been laid out on the pass-through bar, and lawyers and illegals alike dug in. Che and Mitch reached for coffee cups at the same time, but Che stepped back with a deferential bow for the Artotech partner to go first. John Kirk went for another beer, offered Inez and Rafael some. Jake did a double take at the sudden camaraderie. When John Kirk offered him a beer, he politely declined, but accepted a sandwich instead.

"Do you know anything about immigration law?" Will asked Judy.

"Oh, hell, not a lot." Judy straightened her glasses. "I took a course in law school, but that's been—never mind how many years ago." A sheepish look crossed her face.

"Well, maybe it's enough." Will set his glass down. "I mean, you can't just turn these people over to the police. Not after all they've been through."

Mitch frowned. "Now look, we can't change the laws of New Mexico just because of a ...bizarre...set of circumstances."

"Or federal law," John Kirk tossed in.

"These people have been through hell. You may be able to help them," Will persisted. "At least that way some good could come of this."

"A man is dead!" Annike said.

"Sounds like a whole lot more are dead out in the truck and in the road. If these few were spared, maybe it was for some reason. After they've risked their lives, and then pitched in to save all of us, when we hardly lifted a finger to help ourselves—"

"Now wait just a minute," John Kirk said.

Jake cut him off. "It's true. If it wasn't for Ralph here, that *loco* would still be beating your women. Maybe he won't get a medal for it, but something in the way of thanks might be appropriate."

The other man scowled. "Look, if they hadn't tried to crash the country, they wouldn't have been in this situation. This is in no way, shape or form our fault!"

"I ain't blaming you, friend. I'm just saying…" What was the use? Thick heads couldn't be moved without a lot of talk, and Jake didn't have the patience right now. The aspirin had finally taken hold, but what he'd rather have was the bottle of Jack Daniels someone had left on the counter. All of it. And a hot pack for his back and a warm bed.

But it wasn't time yet.

"You're right," Mitch said. "We have to think about this. No one's going to be thinking straight till we calm down and get some rest."

"Exactly." Jake was gratified to finally hear some smart talk out of people who were supposed to be smart, after all. "Where's Will and Zan?" He looked around, finally catching sight of the two at a small table in the lounge. "You two come with me. We'll set up some rooms for the Mexicans. Rest is just what they need."

The trainers dutifully trooped after him, down the wing where their own rooms were, and soon they had enough bunks made up for Inez, Rafael, Che and the other two men.

After they were finished, Jake sent Zanna to get the rooms' intended occupants. They came down, their eyes lighting up at the sight of clean beds. Inez had a bed next to Elsa, who still slept, her pulse a little thready.

"She's gonna have to go to the hospital, friends," Jake said to Rafael and Inez. "I'm sorry. That probably means she's going home."

"She will live?" Inez asked.

"I hope so."

"Then she can try again."

Jake chuckled. "I'll say she can. Maybe in the summer, this time. No snow."

Inez looked puzzled and Rafael translated. "Yes, no snow," they agreed.

Then, to everyone's surprise, the phone rang. Jake limped over to answer it. The state police were on the line. "Yeah, good enough," Jake said. "See you then."

"They're coming?" Will asked.

"They'll be here in five. With Medevac for the wounded. You all get tucked in here and stay quiet, all right? With any luck, they'll come and go without a word to you."

Ralph didn't look convinced, but he took charge of the little bunch and they settled in. Jake asked Will to bring Elsa down the hall to Teo's room, so that both those injured could be removed easily, and hopefully without suspicion of the other illegals hidden down the hall.

With any luck…surely we're entitled to some by now. Seems like we've used up all the bad luck we should have to deal with this week.

He meandered back to the main lounge to make the announcement. "Staties are on their way. Now this is how we're gonna handle things…."

* * * * *

CHAPTER 37

Inez felt like an observer, on the outside, looking in.

In her dream of America, she supposed she had expected she'd be in a community of her peers, and she would have been able to survive knowing as little English as she did. This had not been in her mind.

These people were obviously upper-class, what had Rafael told her? *Notario? Abogado?* Something legal. They were the sort of people she'd be working for, cleaning their house, watching their children, if she ever arrived as expected. At least none of the men had touched her inappropriately here. If the women were cold—some of them—she could understand what was expected of her anyway.

The woman Davi had assaulted was coaxed back to the group by her friends. She spoke to the Mexicans in spurts. Her Spanish was educated and more Castilian, but she warmed up to them, especially to Inez. She even shared some soft sweaters and slacks that must have been her own, because Inez had seen a moment of reluctance in the woman's eyes when she accepted them. The Juarez woman had never owned anything so fine in all her life.

Unable to sleep, she reflected on the nightmarish hours that had passed. She should not judge the others, but she thought her own contribution was morally correct. Her experience at the nursing school had proved useful, and she was grateful that God had allowed her to repay the debt owed to these people who had, however reluctantly, saved her life.

She struggled with the choices before her—what to do, or what would be done with them.

As far as she could tell from the snippets of conversations she had been able to parse out, or what Rafael had told her, a faction of the Americans wanted to help them stay in the country. But at the same time, the *policia* had been called, as was proper, considering those who were gravely injured. Even the sandy-haired man, the *encargado* who Che had beaten, seemed to think they could avoid being taken away, locked up, and then sent home. But she wasn't so optimistic.

With a sigh, she turned to Rafael. "So is that it?"

He appeared skeptical. "I cannot tell. The little one, she seems to say we can have papers, working papers."

"Can she do that?"

"I do not know. Perhaps."

The caretaker returned an hour later with a smile on his face. "Forty-five degrees, ladies and gentlemen," he said. "We're on the home stretch."

"*Que?*" she asked Rafael.

"*Cuarenta cinco. La nieve derretirá.*"

The snow would melt. She sighed. It was coming down to the crucial moments. Once the roads were clear, their fate would be determined.

* * *

"I must be crazy. That's it."

Jake looked at his image in the mirror, realized he hadn't shaved for a couple of days. At least his shirt was clean. The fancy women wouldn't have to be horrified by his hygiene.

Although, he had to admit, the initial reaction he'd seen on their faces five days before at the outwardly scruffy appearance of himself and his *casita* had mellowed considerably. They'd all been through a lot.

But damned if the week hadn't accomplished what Judy Norell had told him it would—they were thinking and acting as a group.

Bet that sure as hell wasn't how they'd thought it would go down.

That thought giving him a little laugh, he pulled on his Cardinals cap and grabbed his keys, shoving them into his jacket pocket. The medevac copter had taken Teo Haroun and the woman Elsa (whose last name he'd never managed to pick up) to Albuquerque for the treatment they needed. The staties had interviewed those in the *casita* about what happened, and every one of them had told the story that hid the fact five Mexicans slept in one of the ranch's back rooms, waiting to see what might happen next. They called for the coroner's truck to start hauling away the bodies, Davi's first.

"I expect the media will be out here soon," one of the officers said to Jake. "You may want to batten down the hatches again."

"I believe you're right. We'll handle it. Thanks."

Jake stood on the front step smiling and waving till they all cleared out. Then he retreated to the office, where Judy and John Kirk were on the phone. They'd used all the connections they had in Denver to finally locate a shelter for illegals in Pueblo, at least a small supportive community where they could remain until legal action could be taken.

At Mitch's direction, they'd also called Pete to come get those not going to the hospital. The plan was coming together.

He walked out to the back patio, where Inez waited. *"¿Cómo va?"* he asked, smiling as the slight woman shone now, her hair brushed and clean, in a cream-colored cashmere sweater that set off her coloring.

Will Starlin ducked from around the back stucco wall with the man identified as Ray and two duffel bags. "This is the last of it, I think. Everyone's been generous."

"Good. They can afford to share."

By the time the staties had arrived, there hadn't been time for Rafael and the others to return to the coyote's truck for their belongings. Maybe when the team got done counting the dead and the possessions, they'd find a discrepancy. But Jake wasn't worried. This little batch would be miles away by then. Meanwhile, he'd shared some of his clothing and personals with Rafael, and the lawyers had done the same for the others.

Jake rubbed his face, acknowledged even the handful of ibuprofen he'd taken hadn't dulled the pain in his back much. He'd have to switch off the driving with those traveling with him to the safe house in Pueblo.

"You sure you don't want me to go with you?" Will offered. "You still don't look good."

Jake clapped him on the shoulder. "I'll manage, son. Got six traveling as it is, even with the extended cab, it'll be a crush. 'Sides, Ralph here drives, right, Ralph?"

Rafael nodded. "Trini also." He helped the others load their bags, including a new Louis Vuitton suitcase that Cattrin had gifted to Inez, in the back of the truck.

"And you're going to the hospital there as soon as you've dropped them off, right?" A hard, determined line in Will's voice warned Jake he'd find a way to come along if Jake didn't promise.

"Yes, son, I'll go. Believe me. I know when I need it." Jake shifted his shoulders just a little to relieve the position they were now held in. Judy and Inez had nearly had to force him to slow down long enough to bandage him tight, in as near a splint as one could make in a mid-back injury, absent a backboard, which he'd refused. "Tell Judy thanks again for the wrap."

"Tell her yourself," came a warm alto from behind him, and the aforesaid lawyer gave him a gentle hug. "The van just pulled up out front."

"Good timing. All right, Ralph, finish loading the truck and I'll be back."

He lumbered through the halls to the front door, Judy following along. The other lawyers and their packed bags awaited.

"We've left the food for you," she said. "Are you sure you don't want us to leave the rest?"

"Absolutely not," he blurted out. At her surprised look, he backpedaled, trying to keep an even demeanor. "I've got my own vices, thanks. You take that with you and we'll all be happy."

"All right. I just wanted to let you know how much we appreciate everything you've done. God knows, this week didn't turn out like any of us expected."

"You can say that again."

The trainers joined them, dragging their equipment boxes on wheels. "I think we got everything," Will said.

"If not, just email me, and I'll send it on, son. Stay in touch, you young-uns." He caught Will's arm just before he got in. "You get that little girl straight. It's a true act of love, son. Either one of you want to talk about it, you give me a call, all right? I'm still in recovery myself, but I know how hard it can be. No matter what time, day or night. You got me?"

Will nodded. "Yes, sir, I will. Thanks for everything."

The spiky-haired young man helped Pete load the baggage on the van. Gradually, each of the lawyers found a seat inside, and all the luggage was stored. Pete slammed the back door closed and came over to Jake.

"You all right, my friend? Word has it some big crap go down here."

"The Lord has his sense of humor, my friend. But we don't get more than we can handle, isn't that what they say?"

Pete's lips twitched into a smile. "Knew this group was trouble from the get-go."

"Aw, they're not so bad. For lawyers."

Pete snorted. "Whatever. You take care now."

"You, too."

Jake stood on the step and watched the van roll down the driveway, taking those guests well enough to travel back to the airport. Once they were out of sight, he walked down the hall, footsteps echoing in the suddenly-empty place. He'd called the usual repair team and left a message for the Shermans. That was one conversation he wasn't looking forward to.

He'd verbalized his worries over losing his job, but Judy reassured him that it wasn't likely.

"It's what we in the legal field call 'exigent circumstances'," Judy said. "Emergency conditions necessary to protect life and limb. We won't file a complaint of any kind—really, we appreciate everything you've done. We wouldn't have made it without you."

"I think we all contributed. Just hope it all turns out right in the end."

Which was why he was bound for Pueblo.

He came out into the fresh air again, locking the door behind him. The skies had cleared, now blue with fluffy white clouds. Spring was back on track.

Jake gestured to the truck. "Saddle up, boys and girls!"

"*Vamonos!*" Rafael added.

When they were all in the truck, their belongings packed in the back, Jake fired up the engine. "It's just a couple of hours, and no snow predicted. We should be just fine. Relax and enjoy the ride."

"*Gracias.*" Inez patted his arm. "You do this for us, it is a small miracle."

"Just paying back some of the grace I've received, hon. You've done the same. It's all we can do is help our fellow man when he needs it."

Jake shut the door with a satisfying metal thunk and they pulled out on the back road heading for U.S. 285. *Well if this don't make me a Boy Scout, guess I'll never get there.*

He chuckled to himself as the tires hit the highway. "So, fellas. Done anything interesting lately?"

* * * * *

CHAPTER 38

Teo woke up in a new place, a bright white place that he thought for that first moment meant he'd crossed over. But gradually, the familiar sounds of a hospital room, beeping monitors, droning televisions, footsteps passing up and down the hallway, all these brought him to reality. Gradually, too, he remembered what had happened out at the ranch, the rough-spoken man who'd shot his way inside the casita and inside Teo's body. The memory brought a wash of cold over him.

"You're awake."

A uniformed nurse in bright flowered scrubs walked in, professional smile on her face. "How are you feeling? Is the pain level under control?"

He realized belatedly he wasn't even feeling pain, everything just a little hazy. Apparently the pain control was working perfectly. He told her so. "Where am I?" he asked through dry lips.

"The University of New Mexico hospital in midtown. You've been here about four days. You didn't need surgery or anything for your injuries, but because of your condition, they agreed to keep you for observation. Your friend has been most insistent that you receive every attention."

The nurse checked his pulse and his temperature and tapped in notes to the laptop computer she carried.

What had she said? A friend? "My friend?" he asked.

"The woman. She's quite a bulldog." The nurse seemed amused.

"Oh. All right." That didn't clarify anything for him, but his puzzlement blended into the haze. "Will the doctor be by sometime soon?"

"Usually late afternoon," the nurse said. "Are you hungry? I can have the kitchen send up a tray."

He considered it. "You know, I think I am."

She nodded with approval. "That's a good sign. I'll send the message from the desk. Is there anything else you need?"

"I...I don't think so. Thanks."

She smiled again and disappeared on her rounds. A few moments later, Cattrin walked in.

"The nurse said you were feeling better, Teo. I'm so glad."

Teo had involuntarily stiffened when he saw her. Surely this wasn't the 'friend' the nurse had referenced. Suspicions ran amuck in his mind.

"Shouldn't you be in Arlington?" he asked.

"I'm right where I should be," she said, pulling a chair close and sitting down next to the bed. "After—the incident—I needed some time off. Mitch has things under control. I wanted to come out here, make sure that you would recover. Of all of us, you deserved this the least."

Teo just stared. *Who was this possessing the malicious Cattrin Odeon? This person sounded almost reasonable. Compassionate. Pleasant, even.*

"I think the experience changed all of us, yes? Perhaps we overlook how others are forced to live. That Che, willing to beat any of us to make sure he had access to food. That man ready to kill you just to sell his fellow human beings for a few hundred dollars in his pocket." She shook her head. "How sad the world has become."

Still skeptical, Teo studied her expression, her calm gaze, seeing nothing of the vicious gossip and social climber he'd known. "What happened? At the ranch?"

She recapped the events after Teo had been shot, concluding with confirmation that the Mexicans had arrived at the shelter, and paperwork was being processed to allow them to stay. "They may need to show they have jobs to go to, now that their journey to St. Louis has been disrupted. But I would guess we could find something for them to do at one of our offices, if nothing else comes through they'd prefer."

Was it the drugs? He could swear this was a hallucination.

When he didn't respond, she just laughed softly. "I know what you're thinking. That I must have flipped my mind. Let's say what happened at the ranch changed me. I've done a lot of thinking. I didn't like who I saw in the mirror of all your faces." She shifted in the chair, her little flutters still very much a part of her. "I'm not perfect, Teo, and I doubt I ever will be. But I want to be a better person. I'm starting with you, because we both know how I've let you down."

'Let him down' was a mild expression, Teo thought. But his own open nature wanted to believe that what she said was true. If she'd really learned something from this week of bizarre events, a change this profound, he should welcome it and receive it in the spirit offered.

"We certainly got our money's worth in the training department this year. Perhaps a little on the dramatic side, though."

"Some of us need a little more work." She reached out to pat his hand. "Can I get you anything?"

"I don't think so. I think everything's going to be all right now."

They'd asked the gods for guidance and change back there at the smudge circle, when the retreat began. They'd received enlightenment and change and so much more.

"Be careful what you wish for," Teo whispered softly. A wave of fatigue coming over him, he closed his eyes, feeling at peace at last. "You might just get it."

THE END

About the Author

Alana Lorens, also writing as Lyndi Alexander, has been a published writer for more than forty years. Currently a resident of North Carolina, she loves her time in the smoky blue mountains. She lives with her daughter, who is the youngest of her seven children, and a few crotchety cats.

* * * * *

Publications by Lyndi Alexander

Horizon Crossover Science Fiction Series:
HORIZON SHIFT (Book I)
HORIZON STRIFE (Book II)
HORIZON DYNASTY (Book III)
SIXSHOOTER (SF Romance)

Science Fiction / Space Opera:
TRIAD

Clan Elves of the Bitterroot Urban Fantasy Series:
THE ELF QUEEN (Book I)
THE ELF CHILD (Book II)
THE ELF MAGE (Book III)
THE ELF GUARDIAN (Book IV)

Young Adult Fantasy:
THE LOST CHORD

* * * * *

www.ingramcontent.com/pod-product-compliance
Lightning Source LLC
Chambersburg PA
CBHW032213170626
46808CB00006B/2448